CORNERED!

Two of the scavengers raced toward Stone. They were huge, leather-faced things, with spikes where teeth should have been, their bodies covered with immense, badly sewn buffalo hides. One was swinging a long axe; the other was twirling some kind of hook-like weapon that he swung on the end of a spiked chain. Stone watched the orbiting hook coming in toward his chest like a meathook. He launched himself forward...

*   *   *

THE RABID BRIGADIER

ALSO BY CRAIG SARGENT

The Last Ranger
The Savage Stronghold
The Madman's Mansion
The War Weapons*

Published by
POPULAR LIBRARY   *forthcoming

THE RABID BRIGADIER

CRAIG SARGENT

POPULAR LIBRARY

An Imprint of Warner Books, Inc.

A Warner Communications Company

CHAPTER
One

SOMEONE WAS about to die.

He awoke with a start, sitting bolt upright. The hairs on the back of his neck were standing up like little quills. Where was he? How long had he been asleep? It seemed as if he had just been in a black funnel, a storm of darkness deep and twisting, swirling down into unfathomable regions. He knew that if he hadn't awakened right then —just a moment before the cloud swallowed him, a second before the funnel swept him up in its wispy clenching jaws —that he would never have awoken. For there was blood in the air. Murder all around him.

He looked around sharply, trying to ascertain his location. It was night but the full sky of stars spread out across the heavens like a mess of spilled marbles and a thick bloated moon sitting directly overhead he could see clearly. There was rubble everywhere and bodies. Suddenly he remembered the explosion that he had set, and then the storm of smoking rock and dismembered flesh falling from the black sky; all that was left of the Dwarf's fortress and vacation retreat for the high-rolling criminals of America. A small smile sketched its way across his ash-coated face. At least he had accomplished something in this hellhole, tipped the scales of blackness and light ever so slightly to the side away from the darkness.

It all came back to him—the truck he had escaped in, then the roaring eruption, the truckload of whores who dug him out. He had just put his head down to rest for a moment, and . . . he must have just passed out on the spot. The whores were nowhere to be seen. Just bodies all around him as if the sky had rained flesh, had cried blood.

He heard a noise off in the shadows, then another and the smile vanished from his mouth like a fish darting back into the darker waters. Figures were rushing around the debris like rats, bent over, furtive. They mouthed obscene laughs as they searched the dead bodies for booty, rifling through the bloodstained clothes with quick, filthy fingers, grabbing everything that was still usable—boots, jewelry, knives, whatever. Martin Stone dropped back down to the center of the small explosion-created crater he was lying in and watched with drawn breath.

Suddenly he heard a coarse voice perhaps ten yards off. "Found me a good one," it yelled. Then there was the slicing sound of a knife sawing through flesh. Stone raised his head slowly and peered out over the rise . . . and almost puked up what little food was still sitting in his stomach from his last meal two days before. For one of the scavengers was cutting off the ears of a body on the ground, its long dead hands clasped together in a prayer of rigor mortis. He cut away with a long hunting knife with the expertise of someone who had carried out the action numerous times, rising with the two red dripping appendages in his hand.

"Got me two more," the scabby creature yelled to his pals, who were busy on their hands and knees filling burlap sacks with everything they could find that would be of use to their miserable lives. Stone could see through the moonlight filtering down through high curtains of cloud that the man was hideously ugly, his face misshapen and scarred as if he had been through a meat grinder more than once. And he saw something else—a necklace of ears around the scavenger's neck, shrunken to the size of dried apricots, hard and brown. There must have been a hundred of them, extending clear around the man's stubbled throat. The human slime held the bloody ears up in the air examining the newest additions to his necklace of human flesh by the rays of the neon moon.

"Jesus Christ," Stone mumbled under his breath. So many people had died to create the bastard's grotesque jewelry. It wasn't how he felt like ending up, that was for damned sure. He felt down to his waist, reaching frantically for his .44 — but it was gone. His knife was missing too. The whores had stripped him of everything that could kill. He searched around with darting bloodshot eyes for anything that he could use to fight with. For the corpse strippers were drawing closer by the second, and they were heading right toward him.

"Lookee here," the ear cutter laughed out with sputtering glee through his half toothless mouth. "Another! Got me another set. Damn, if I ain't gonna need to start a new necklace soon." He bent down over the body of a woman, and sliced down hard twice. Two more ears fell free, the gaping holes in the skull gushing out a red liquid ooze that coated the slicer's filth-coated boots. But he didn't seem to notice

or care as he moved ahead searching for more. Tonight he
was in paradise—a Garden of Eden of death.

Stone dropped down flat on his back as the scavenger
walked up to the dusty crater and saw him lying there.

"Look at this one; don't even look hurt," the cutter yelled
to his pals, who moved across the field of bodies like locusts
stripping a forest. "His ears are perfect . . . like uncut
diamonds . . . big ones too. This is my goddamned night.
Lady fucking luck is looking over my shoulder." He kneeled
down and raised the knife to bring it down on Stone's right
ear, but before the long blade could descend, the would-be
corpse threw a handful of dust into the man's face. Coughing
and momentarily blinded, the cutter fell backwards, landing
on his ass as he tried to wipe the grit free from his eyes with
snot-covered cuffs.

Stone was upon him like a leopard on an impala. He
kicked the slime in the face, catching him directly under the
chin and the big man's mouth erupted in a spurt of blood.
Stone grabbed the gnarled hand and twisted it hard, grabbing
the knife as it fell free. But the others had heard the struggle
and suddenly appeared out of the shadows, surrounding him.
Without hesitation Stone jumped behind the ear cutter,
grabbed a handful of greasy, lice-infested hair, and pulled
back hard. He rammed the blade edge against the Adam's
apple and pulled the man to his feet.

"Back off, slime, or he's dead," Stone screamed, suddenly able to see as he rose just how many of this happy
crew there were. Too many! There must have been nearly a
dozen of them, their burlap bags filled with rotting treasures
as they stared with wide open mouths at him. Corpses
weren't supposed to fight back. But if that's what tonight's
little game was going to be, so be it. With something approaching the pleasurable look a gourmet gets on his face

when he sits down to a meal of steaming escargots, they gently set their bags down on the debris-covered ground and pulled out an assortment of weapons—knives, axes, meat hooks—to greet their uninvited guest.

Stone gulped hard and pushed ear cutter forward, keeping the knife right against the jugular, ready to dig in deep if the bastard made the slightest move. But he didn't. Like all scum, he was brave only when he had the upper hand. Stone prayed that the man was the leader of the group, or at least in the upper echelon, or the rest of them would only see it as an opportunity to get yet more treasure by taking them both out.

But apparently earman was high in the pecking order, for the smiles vanished from the scavenger crew's face as they realized that their pal was in big trouble.

"What should we do, Ear?" the scavenger closest to Stone, with a pockmarked face, nose half eaten away as if it had worms in it, screamed in something approaching hysteria.

"Just . . . just take it easy, boys," the prisoner stuttered back. "This man don't mean no harm, do you, fellow? He just thought I meant him harm, which I didn't. How the hell was I supposed to know you wasn't dead?" he beseeched Stone. "Just lemme go and you can walk. I swear."

"Kill him," one of the corpse strippers yelled, coming toward Stone from the right holding a machete in his raised hand. "If we all charge, we'll cut the bastard up into ant food."

"No! No!" Stone's prisoner yelled back even louder. "Don't one of you make a move, you hear me. If you do— and he cuts me—I'll get you, if I have to come back from the grave." Such was the awe in which the others held Ear that they stopped in their tracks and made room for Stone, who moved slowly through their ranks, gripping his stinking Get-Out-of-Jail-Free-Card with every bit of strength in his sore arms. The ranks opened like the Red Sea parting and though Stone could see by their grinding jaws and wild eyes that there was nothing they wanted more on this earth than to say hello to his kidneys with their blades, they held back.

He was just beginning to think he might actually make it when Ear decided to make a move. He grabbed Stone's knife hand with both of his steel fists and bit down hard with the few teeth that remained in his mouth, the cracked fangs sinking deep into the back of Stone's hand. Stone let out a howl of pain but he didn't drop the blade. Ripping the hand free of the man's jaws, he slammed the knife back again, ripping it across the thick throat. The flesh parted like butter as the razor-sharp edge dug in deep, cutting muscle and artery in a flash. Stone pushed the dying thing away from him as it spewed out a waterfall of red, the mouth gurgling out a wet sickening sound as blood gushed from between his lips instead of words. He fell forward, hands wrapped around his own throat as if he was trying to hold it all back in.

Out of the frying pan into hell. As if the cutting of Ear's throat were the signal to charge, the rest of the slime rushed toward Stone with murder in their black eyes. Stone ran straight toward the closest one, remembering his late father's, Major Clayton Stone's words: "Never run away; charge when the shit hits the fan. At least it gives you a split second of surprise." The noseless slime was coming at Stone, his machete raised high overhead in his right hand ready to deal a death blow . . . but Stone struck paydirt first. He came in fast from the left and slammed the blade into the man's guts, slicing it from left to right so the entire stomach opened up. He ripped it out just as fast and stepped to the side. The machete wielder stopped as if he'd run into a brick wall, his mouth twitching as if he'd just swallowed a rattle-snake. He looked down at the spreading red across his deer-hide jacket, at his own intestines sliding out from his stomach, releasing a load of half digested food and blood, and his eyes got a look of infinite surprise.

"I—I can't die," he blurted out as if making a confes-sional to Stone. "I've killed them all. Everyone I've fought."

"No comment," Stone spat out, grabbing the machete from the trembling stiffened hand. He turned and rushed into the melee without a backward glance at the dying man whose eyes were glued to his rushing guts as if he were looking into the punishing face of God himself. With a blade in each hand Stone waded into the next two takers like a tank going into a crumbling fence.

They were tough but they weren't fast. Not fast enough, anyway, as they found out. With his youth and training and lean-muscled body Stone was suddenly somehow right be-tween the two of them, slipping down on both knees as their blades stabbed forward. He ripped the machete and the bowie-sized hunting blade into each man's knee, cutting right through the bone and slicing the thick connecting tissue inside into broken wires that no longer supported their part of the load. As they tumbled forward, each man's wounded leg falling limp as wet tissue, and slammed into the ground, Stone was already up and moving, rising to his feet in a single leaping motion as he propelled himself forward into the charging wild-eyed ranks that seemed to have no end.

Stone tried to calm himself and be objective as he started forward toward the next three, their steel blades and axes caught for a split second by an errant beam of the moon, flashing into his eyes with a telegram of death. He didn't have to kill all of them, for Christ's sake, he thought to

himself as he suddenly changed direction in mid-stride, pulling them off balance for a second. Just get through them, to
the road ahead. He could outrun them there. There was just
this three, and then two beyond them. *It was a football
game, that's all,* he tried to bullshit himself, *and I'm the
ball.*

Plan made, Stone came straight toward the three rather
anxious individuals who were zeroing in on his body like it
was Christmas roast, and again feinted to the right, so that
all three of them veered that way. Like a receiver in full
stride, he turned his leg and pushed off with the right foot,
suddenly spinning him away from them again, catapulted by
the force of the motion like a ricocheting rock. He swung the
machete forward as he spun by the closest of the scavengers,
a man with a long black beard that reached almost to his
stomach and a mat of twisted hair piled high on his head.
The motion was so quick that none of them quite realized
what had happened for a second. Stone just suddenly was
gone—and then the two scavengers turned and saw their pal
with his hands to his face screaming, or trying to scream.

For the machete had gone point first into the opened
mouth of the man, cutting all the way into his throat and out
the back of his neck. It was as if he was a sword swallower,
only he wasn't. His eyes rolled back in his head, looking
like overcooked eggs about to burst their shells as the man
tried to scream. But with the blade filling his entire oral
cavity it was a little difficult. A gush of liquid swam out
from all sides of the machete as his severed jugular vein fed
out a stream of red through his lips. He looked as if he was
one of those statues rich people or would-be's had on their
lawn, spitting out a little fountain of water. Only this was
blood.

His black beard turned red, bright red, red as Santa's

Christmas hat, and gurgling pink bubbles of foam he fell forward. The handle of the blade slammed butt-end first into the dirt, pushing with all the weight of the scavenger's two-hundred-seventy pounds plus into the machete, pushing the blade in a kind of circular motion. The sharp edge sliced through everything that was left and the entire head pulled free of the body, somehow still horribly alive—eyes rolling, quivering lips whispering moans of incredible pain.

But Stone was long gone. The moment he felt the machete dig in he let go of it and shot forward. The remaining two, huge leather-faced things, with spikes where teeth should have been, their frames covered over in immense, badly sewn buffalo hides that still stank of bison urine, came toward him. One was swinging a long axe, the other twirling a hooklike weapon that he swung on the end of a spiked chain. Just the kind of guys you'd like to go bowling with. Stone watched the orbiting hook coming in toward his chest like a meat hook searching for meat to sink into and timed himself. As the orbit just took it by, he launched himself straight toward the bearer. By the time the hook spun around again, Stone was already inside the man's reach. He caught the inside of the hook with his left hand as he slammed his knife hand up and inside right between the man's legs.

The scavenger seemed to shoot like a rocket into the blood-scented air as his genitals exploded from his body. He had the most terrified expression Stone had ever seen on a man. Stone grabbed the handle of the hook as it fell from the air. The wood-cutting axe of the attacker bit into the dirt just inches from his foot as Stone let the hook go toward the man's chest.

The tip of the hook caught the flesh scavenger just beneath the rib cage and as soon as he felt it dig in, Stone pulled back hard like a fisherman landing a bass. The eight

inch hook dug deep up and under the ribs, hooking into the
right lung. Stone stepped back another yard, pulled on the
chain as the man came helplessly forward, walking as if on
his toes, as he sucked in hard for air. Stone wrapped both
forearms around the chain and pulled with every once of
strength. The hook ripped forward and tore right through the
rib cage of the man, exploding in a tidal wave of blood and
lung and whatever the hell else is stuck up there inside the
chest. It was as if a bomb had gone off inside him. He
toppled forward like a tree pouring blood and lay there quivering and letting out sounds that sounded like the mews of a
dying kitten.

Stone rose to his feet and raised the knife hand, ready for
the next man. And still they came toward him, howling in
mad rage even after seeing six of their number slaughtered
like cattle. The son-of-bitches were stupid or brave. Maybe
they were the same fucking thing, Stone thought disgustedly.
But he didn't have to fight them anymore. The road lay just
ahead. Dark, snow-covered, but he could beat them in a flat
race. He turned in a flash and shot into the dancing shadows
as the moon flickered in and out of the darkening clouds
overhead, creating a kaleidoscope of rippling ribbons of
darkness and light. They lumbered after him, screaming,
enraged, swinging their slicers with wild flailing arms. They •
came down the road in their stinking furs and thick coats of
handmade armor from wired-together rows of tin cans like a
herd of mastodons who didn't know they were already extinct. But Stone was gone, disappearing into the darkness.
They kept on for almost fifty yards, with a lot of huffing and
puffing just for face's sake. Then they stopped.

CHAPTER
Two

IF DOGS can pray then this one was praying with all the fervor of its canine heart, praying a message of supreme thanks that Martin Stone was walking toward it from out of the mist-shrouded forests. The bull terrier had begun to think that he was never coming back, that he was gone, or dead. It had greedily eaten all its food and water within the first few hours of his departure. Subsequently it had had nothing for days while it stayed hidden in the thick bush where Stone had left it and the Harley. But now he was here. It would drink. It would eat.

Its eyes grew big as creampuffs and it whined out a shrill childlike screech as its muscular white body trembled wildly. Suddenly, as if unable to contain its enthusiasm, the bull terrier jumped high in the air, twisting around in a corkscrew motion like a dolphin spinning in water. Stone couldn't help but laugh and grabbed the dog around the collar, pulling it toward him so it slammed into his chest, bounced off him,

hit the ground and then shot right back up again like a cue
ball looking for a game of billiards. It put its paws on his
chest and sniffed him with a strange expression. Stone
looked down and saw that he was covered from just below
the neck to mid-thigh with blood and specks of purple flesh.
The dog sniffed hard again and then jumped down to the
ground in disgust. Good, Stone thought. Excaliber wouldn't
lick human blood. He didn't want it to ever acquire a taste
for homo sapiens or a hell of a lot of people would be missing tails, and other things. But the bull terrier was smart; it
knew that mankind was too bitter a steak to chew.

"Yeah, I'm here. Master is back." The dog whined greedily, its nose aiming up toward the canteen on his waist.
Stone took it off and the fighting dog let its huge tongue slap
out of its mouth several times in restless anticipation. Stone
reached down and poured a stream of the cool liquid into the
animal's empty bowl. Its face hit the stuff with a splash and
it began lapping away madly so that only about half the
water actually made it into its throat. But it was the idea that
counted, and it looked up happily after about a minute of
machinelike licking.

Stone grunted hard as he lifted the huge Harley 1200cc
Electraglide from its side, hidden in the center of a doughnut
of thick shrubs. It was hard going pushing the mobile battle-
wagon through the wooden tendrils that grabbed everywhere
with thorny fingers. But after about five minutes he pulled it
free, out onto a deer path, and mounted up.

"Come on, dog. We gotta get out of here before some of
my recent acquaintances come looking for more action."
Stone patted the thick leather seat behind him on the pur-
ring bike and Excaliber looked over from where he was
sniffing a dark, fungi-covered wet log, nosing around for
black beetles. Suddenly the pitbull found one and

snapped it into his jaws. He crunched hard, popping the armor shell like a peanut, and swallowed it with a look of gourmet delight. Then he turned and ran, reaching the Harley in two quick strides. Without breaking step the bull terrier jumped and landed smoothly on the back, gripping its front and back legs around the sides of the seat like a starfish wrapped around a clam. Stone looked down at his hand. It was throbbing painfully, the top of it red and swelling already. The teethmarks of Ear's few molars were clear on the flesh. It was infected with that slime's mucus. God only knew what kind of diseases Stone was going to get now.

He reached around behind him on the bike into the medical box, quickly took out and rubbed on Ampicillin and Tetracycline Salve over the wound and then popped down some pills of the same. His father had prepared, among many things, a number of combat-usable ointments and medicines —just a few tricks he had picked up in his twenty years fighting in Southeast Asia and Latin America. How it would work against human saliva was another question.

Stone pulled back the accelerator on the handlebar and the bike picked up speed along an ice and snow patched road that headed quickly up into the lower slopes of the Uinta Mountains, Utah. Dr. Kennedy, the double-talking, snake oil salesman extraordinaire who had helped get him into the now decimated Last Resort, had also been able to get out with Stone's sister April just minutes before Stone sent the place into a smoking hell. He trusted the man with his life. Kennedy must have run into trouble, and had to split fast. There had been enough guards after them all back there. He wouldn't let himself think for even one second that they hadn't made it. No way. No fucking way. But where would he have headed?

Stone slowed as the bike approached a steep road that

angled sharply up and around in a long twisting motion, up the side of a towering mountain. The night seemed to grow darker by the minute as thick rolling storm clouds filled the heavens above, a churning sea of mile-wide fists that threatened to pummel the earth at any moment. Rangely—that was it. Kennedy had mentioned that he used Rangely for his base in this part of the country. A place where he had friends—people who would hide him. It was about sixty miles to the east, which Stone knew would be closer to one hundred and twenty or more through these twisted mountains and valleys. He exhaled a breath of deep weariness and sped up slightly as the dog barked for a second, as if feeling his master's anxieties.

Stone rode through the night seeming to ascend forever into the mountains, into the very heavens, which twisted in a sea of black that and felt like just yards above his head. The moisture condensed down from above in sheets of gray, filling the slopes with a thick cold mist that coated him and the dog with a cloak of liquid. Even with the deep grooved tires of the Harley, Stone had to take it easy on the ice-sheened one-lane road, the edge of which dropped thousands of feet to a chasm of rock-hard teeth ready to smash anything that came hurtling down into pudding. The bike's headlight burnt a dim hole through the icy fog, just enough for Stone to edge on into the darkness.

At last they reached the peak. Though he couldn't see it, Stone could feel the ground level off fairly rapidly, go on for about two hundred feet then start down again. Moving slow as a turtle, Stone eased the big bike down the far slope, absurdly slow for a machine of that size and capability. But if they went over the edge, it wouldn't be anything but twisted junk. And so its power was reined in as Stone kept both feet on the icy road, just sliding along down the side.

Suddenly he sucked in, a breath of awe. For they had dropped instantly out of the cloud level. And below, as far as the eye could see, was a fairyland of hills and streams, low valleys and darkly colored geometric shapes of fields and small towns. The moon sliced through the cloud cover several miles off, sending down a stream of white beams that lit the terrain with a brilliant merciless light. He felt for a split second as if he could see all the world, melting into weaving shadows at the end of the horizon.

Another wave of weariness swept over him. And this time he could hardly fight it. His knees felt like they were about to buckle beneath him. His body hurt bad from the force of the explosion the day before. He had been trying to deny it, but some of his joints felt as if they could hardly move anymore. He had to rest, to eat. He hadn't eaten for days. He saw a sudden outcrop that came right out of the mountainside—a plateau several hundred yards wide with a band of dense shrubs covering the edge, creating a natural windbreak. Stone pulled the bike off the road and across the wide ledge to the far side, away and unseen from the road. He turned the engine off and the night was suddenly eerily quiet.

He stepped off the bike and the autorest popped out from the side, letting the bike sink onto its wide metal foot. Stone pulled out a tarp from one of many black alloy cases that were fitted in racks around the back. Pulling out two collapsible tent poles, he quickly erected what would pass for a small lean-to and then pulled down the flaps on both sides so that they and the entire bike were virtually enclosed. Already it seemed a little warmer, with the ice-edged night air held at bay by the ripstop nylon walls. The pitbull awoke suddenly from where it had been sleeping on and off on the back seat and sat up, staring at Stone from the top of the Harley.

"After the work's done the wonderdog awakens. As usual," Stone said, giving a halfhearted evil eye to the canine, which yawned so wide that Stone was sure the animal's jawbone would snap apart at the seams. But the sharklike jaws clamped loudly shut again and the dog looked at Stone with its inscrutable almond eyes, and whined intently. "Well, you woke too soon, pal. The work's not all done." Stone opened one of the survival cases stacked on the back of the bike and took out a small stove. He turned a knob and the gas heater/stove lit instantly, sending out a reassuring wave of heat through the makeshift shelter. Placing it on the ground, Stone warmed his hands over it for a minute, trying to get his joints and knuckles a little bit looser. He washed them in the heat, rubbing the hands from palms out, down the fingers, trying to shake off the pain and injury.

Opening a long rectangular box in the lower part of the rack system, Stone extracted the stock of a .30 caliber marksman's rifle. He took the various broken-down pieces from their hard foam beds and fitted the entire long range rifle system together in a couple of minutes. Then the sighting system—infrared—was screwed onto the top of the weapon's ring system. It had been designed originally to kill Russians, but it would kill everything else just as well.

"Come on, dog," Stone said, pulling the flap aside. "Those who work, eat; those who don't, starve. Or haven't you read your Karl Marx today?" The fighting animal followed right along at his heels, knowing instinctively that nutrition was involved. Stone walked about fifteen yards to a rock overhang that looked out across the mountain plateau and onto groves of trees growing up from the slopes that surrounded it. He rested himself on his stomach and elbows, got the dog quieted down and still beside him, and sighted up through the telescopic view on top. He flicked a small black switch and the power unit of the infrared detector hummed on. The whole world came to life in a bizarre pattern of red and orange dancing waves of light. He saw things by their heat patterns now, the birds breathing hard in the trees, owls, and rodents along the ground. With the cool air around them, the heat of living matter seemed to burn like little red suns against the cold blue background.

There—movement. A jackrabbit. Stone followed it as it hopped madly across an open space and he eased his finger down on the trigger. The autosilencer built into the muzzle released a harsh hiss as the .30 caliber slug spun free and through the night air. In a fraction of a second it tore into the rabbit, sending it flying in a heap of spinning fur up into the sky like something aiming for space flight. Then it came down again hard in a reddish-looking heap and didn't move.

"Go!" Stone commanded, pointing at the downed prey. He stared over at the pitbull, which stared back. "Fetch, get that fucking rabbit—that's dinner! Go! Go!" Stone commanded it in his most stern tones, but the pitbull just looked at him as if he was crazy. Then it sniffed the air coming from the dead animal and came up on all fours. The ninety-pound satchel of steel grace leapt six feet from the ledge they were on and began running at full speed across the open field. Stone watched the heat blur of the dog as it moved like a panther toward the fading orange glow of the rabbit. Excaliber picked up the cottontail and set it carefully beneath his canines, hardly pressing down at all, and took off again back toward Stone. He came to a skidding halt before the rock and, resting on his haunches, the bull terrier launched itself back up onto the rock ledge. Its front paws made it but its back ones didn't and they clawed frantically against the rock with a horrible kind of scratching sound that a fingernail makes when scraped on a blackboard. Stone reached down and grabbed hold of the flailing animal around the chest and pulled it up with a heave.

"Good boy," Stone said when the dog was at last planted on terra firma again. The pitbull dropped the prey at his feet. It was a monster of a rabbit, as big as he'd ever seen—what was left of it. For the .30 caliber slug had taken its head clean off. But what was left was plenty. Even for the two of them.

CHAPTER
Three

WHEN STONE stepped outside the tarp the next morning the sky was still black as night and churning with a malevolent fury. He wouldn't have known it was daytime but for the dim ashen face of the sun straight off on the horizon, barely able to burn its shape through the ceiling of clouds. Something was in the offing, something bad. The bull terrier trotted out next to him, took one look, turned and walked back inside.

"Yeah, you got the right idea," Stone muttered as he spat a thick gob of sleep-collected phlegm onto the snow-speck-led ground. "Unfortunately, we got promises to keep." He pulled the tarp down and folded it up, stowing it in back of the Harley. Excaliber, lying contentedly next to the front wheel of the bike, was suddenly exposed to the cold biting wind that seemed to sweep across the slope as if bidding them good morning. He stood up, looked at Stone with nasty eyes and then shook his whole body, sending a wave of warm blood coursing through his veins. The pitbull stretched forward and back, pulling his legs as far as they would go in each direction in some canine version of yoga and then jumped up to the back seat where he waited mouth open, drool slobbering down onto the leather.

Stone started up the buffalo-sized Harley. He put the motorcycle in gear and headed across the plateau, then back out onto the mountain road, if it could be called that. It had been five years since America had for all intents and purposes stopped being a society and started falling toward the barbarism that was the new "civilization." The roads were the first to go, cracked, asphalt bubbling up like stew cooked too long on the stove of the eternal sun. He was glad he had the Harley. Any kind of four-wheel vehicle would have found the going virtually impossible.

With the thick mist gone on the lower slopes of the mountain Stone was able to open up full throttle once he felt fully awake. He still felt strange, though. The hand where he had been bitten was swollen with a huge boil now. But though he could feel it he wouldn't look at it. There wasn't a hell of a lot he could do about it, so he chose to ignore it, hoping that whatever was going on in there would go away. But it hurt like the blazes, throbbing beneath the skin as if something was alive in there, something diseased and growing.

They hit the bottom of the mountain after about an hour and a long plain spread out ahead flat as a pane of glass, and at the far end, perhaps twenty miles off, another range of mountains rose out of the brown earth like granite arms reaching for the sky. He stopped the Harley at the very edge of the flatlands and rested his feet on the ground, staring up hard at the heavens. It was getting worse up there, not better. The sky seemed to be alive, filled with churning clouds, like a pit of black serpents all writhing and sliding among one another. The air was so thick with moisture he felt he could open his mouth and drink. Yet the rains didn't fall. It was as if the clouds were holding it all back, wanting to fill the creatures below with fear and trembling, wanting to eke every ounce of apprehension from the life forms that inhabited the prairie before they actually released their torrents. Stone debated for several minutes whether to go on. If he got caught out there and it came, there could be flash floods, sheets of water driving across the plain like a tidal wave. But he couldn't wait. In the new America, there was no waiting —for anything. The slow were lost, died, eaten, whatever. If nothing else, Stone knew that one fact beyond all else. The new world was not a place for the indecisive.

He pulled back on the accelerator and tore onto the flat, fissured terrain without glancing back. Within minutes they were cruising along the hard-packed flats at a good 60mph. Excaliber tried to do his usual deep sleep routine but the bull terrier sensed the danger above and its eyes kept popping open to glance upward at the sky. At last the animal sat up, back legs still wrapped for dear life around the seat, front legs extended up so it was sort of half standing, leaning against Stone's back, and stared dead ahead at the rushing landscape.

For a wasteland the countryside was amazingly filled with life. Animals seemed to whiz by them, browsing among the snow-jeweled vegetation, trying to get what nourishment they could from the winter terrain. Bison, deer, moles, lizards all jerked and ran away from the roar of the bike, stopping some yards off when they saw it meant them no harm. Then they returned to their search with radar eyes for anything edible. Excaliber let out an occasional bark or two as he spotted some furry creature or other scampering off, but it was obviously more of a friendly morning greeting than a threat to leap from the bike and into the fray. It was other dogs that seemed to get his goat, as if he had to show them just who was boss. But for the moment anyway, there was nothing out there doglike enough to get the English pitbull's juices flowing.

They had gone for about an hour when Stone noticed a large shape ahead of them, about thirty yards to the right. It piqued his curiosity, since it seemed to be the skeleton of a quite immense animal, rib bones poking through a coating of sand and coarsely textured red stone. He stopped the Harley, stepped off and walked over to the object, the pitbull jumping around his heels as it took full advantage of the momentary stop to get some blood going through its cramped muscles. Stone whistled as he made a full circumference of the long dead creature. It was huge. No way it could be a bison, even a mutant one. The rib cage of the thing looked like it could have held a small car. The head, half submerged in the ground, was covered with several inches of coagulated mud, and Stone whipped out his foot, kicking the substance free. His eyes opened even wider—it was a dinosaur. A triceratops if his high school memories of biology class were accurate. That huge armored head and triple horns were unmistakable. This thing hadn't been dead a few months— more like one hundred million years. Suddenly he realized that he must be in a section of the Dinosaur National Park, in eastern Utah—where archaeologists had been digging up dinosaur bones for decades.

Stone felt a sense of awe fill his heart as he walked around the thing, examining it closely, trying to feel what it had been like to have lived back then. Excaliber grabbed a piece of rib that had fallen to the dirt and took a deep grinding chew on the thing. Then with an expression of unmistakable revulsion it spat the primeval meal out again, coughing and sputtering like it'd just eaten a mouthful of dust. Which it had. For the bones, although still maintaining their basic shape, were already starting to decompose upon exposure to the air. They had been buried for eons, uncovered just weeks before by a severe windstorm. And now they waited to disappear into the acidic oxygen atmosphere of the earth forever.

Stone felt tears welling in his eyes, which was just about the most ridiculous thing he could imagine. Crying over something that had died before the first monkey was born. But it wasn't the creature itself, it was . . . memories. Memories of going to the museum with his father, Major Clayton, when he was just a child. How he had loved the giant lizards, as all children do, feeling an inexplicable, almost mystical attraction to the impossible creatures. And now that was all gone—gone forever most likely. Museums, his father, children with wide excited eyes carrying balloons. All gone, as this thing was. Dead, buried, extinct. And perhaps the most frightening thought—which he would barely allow himself to think—that the human race was heading down the same road, the highway to non-existence. And soon all that would be left of the entire species would be little rises in the desert containing the ivory bones of the homo sapiens.

Knowing the thing would completely vanish before the winter was over, Stone broke off a little fragment from the top of the horn in the center of the dinosaur's head. He looked down into the empty eye sockets, behind which was just blackness, and issued an apology.

"Sorry, pal, don't mean to mutilate you or anything, but it's done out of love, I swear. Besides, no doubt I'll be joining you soon enough and you can give me a piece of your mind." He tucked the three-inch fragment inside his camouflage jacket pocket and turned back to the bike.

Excaliber, who had been poking his face around the rib cage
—to see if there was anything worth chewing—nearly
caught his head and had to pull frantically to get free. After
about ten seconds of growling struggle he gave an extra hard
pull and two of the six-foot-long curved rib bones snapped
like wishbones as the pitbull fell backwards to the ground.
Stone, who hadn't even seen the little drama, just sat back
on the bike and glanced around to see the fighting dog leaping onto the seat, coated with the white chalky dust of another age. He started up.

If it was possible, the sky seemed to be growing ever
darker as if the entire heavens were falling onto the earth,
ready to bury them all. And as if the sky was reading his
thoughts Stone heard a deep rumble from above that seemed
to pass across the entire horizon with such a powerful subsonic vibration that its echo was felt through his bones.

Then the first drop fell, landing square on his nose. Then
another. And within seconds the deluge began. Rain poured
from the skies like it had never rained before. Sheets and
torrents of liquid ripping down with such velocity that it
stung his face like little darts slapping against his skin. He
had never seen so much water fall so suddenly. It was more
like a waterfall had opened up over them than a rain storm.
It was as if the clouds wanted to destroy what lay below
them, and the curtains of silver liquid slammed down,
punching a million little craters into the hard ground.

Stone kept the bike going but had to slow to about twenty
mph since he could only see about ten yards ahead. The dog
let out a howl of unhappiness and Stone looked around to
see a waterlogged mop of a creature staring at him with
consternation.

"Hang on, pal," he yelled back from the corner of his

mouth, almost gagging as the falling rain rushed into his mouth. "Can't get any worse, right?" But he was wrong about that too; the storm was just starting to feel its oats.

The sky just ignited with streaks of yellow and white, spider webs of jagged million-volt fire spreading out across the sky and down to the earth. The landscape all around him seemed to take a hundred hits, as if bombs were being dropped by a hidden armada. Cacti, trees, boulders—all took jolts of the electric bombardment and were no more. Stone could hardly hear the drone of the bike as the thunder was constant now, like a hydrogen bomb going off forever, and the striking lightning sent out its own deafening roars as it decimated everything that it touched.

There was nothing to do except hang on, and keep the Harley going. He prayed the bike wouldn't take a direct hit, or it would be all over. But though the bolts of white seemed to hit everywhere around the Electraglide, they didn't make contact with the machine. The rain continued unabated, growing in intensity as Stone headed the bike across the flatlands like a waterlogged turtle. And as the falling rain collected in dips and gulleys in the ground, the bike seemed to sink down every few seconds as if it were fording rivers rather than crossing the usually parched terrain. The thick wheels of the bike sent out a spray of mud behind them and sometimes up onto them. A low howl emitted from Excaliber's wet throat and wouldn't stop. Long and drawn and quite unhappy. And mixed in with the thunder, the lightning, the whistling roar of the rain, it all made for quite a cacophonous chorus.

"Fuck!" Stone screamed into the wind, deciding to join in with his own contribution. This was ridiculous. But as there was no turning back and he didn't feel like lying in the dirt and drowning at that moment, he just kept on, hunched over the front of the bike, his thick jacket pulled up around his shoulders and neck as high as it would go. The image of the warmth and comfort of the bunker that his father had built, where Martin and his family had spent the last five years, suddenly filled his mind like a vision of paradise. The idea of sleeping on a warm dry bed felt akin to entering heaven, and he kept it in the forefront of his consciousness like a kind of carrot to lure him on.

Suddenly they hit something, he didn't know what, and he didn't have much time to think about it, for the Harley lurched violently and shot into the air, turning sideways. Stone felt himself flying right off the seat and into the air like some kind of wingless bird. The only thing he could think was not to let the bike fall on him, or it would all be over. He somehow managed to twist his body so he took off away from the bike, which was going all the way over just to his left, upside down. He hit the ground hard, but the water cover and his instinctive reactions helped him hit on a roll. He felt himself somersaulting over and over through the rain and then skidded another few yards, almost hydroplaning along the surface. He stopped and lay there for a second, not moving, to make sure nothing was broken. But aside from feeling bruised as hell, he felt more or less intact. He slowly rose, dripping mud and water like a swamp creature, and looked around, suddenly alarmed that the dog might have been crushed.

"Excaliber? Hey dog, where the fuck are you?" Stone screamed through the rain, cupping his hands over his grime-coated mouth. An angry bark came from beneath the swirls of rain and Stone walked a few yards to the dog, which was standing in a puddle that came up to its shoulders glaring at him.

It stomped out of the mini-lake, walked over to him until it stood at his feet and shook itself violently, sending out a spray of mist into the air. Stone let out a watery laugh. The two of them looked about as pitiful as two living creatures could get. The pitbull didn't seem to see the humor of the situation and squinted its almond-shaped eyes. If looks could kill Stone was dead.

"Come on, dog, you needed a bath anyway," he said and walked over to the bike. It lay on its side, lodged halfway through a small brown cactus that it had nearly severed. He got down on his knees and peered anxiously at the wheels. But they were unbent. Thank God the engine was totally enclosed, virtually watertight. His father had foreseen that the going might be a little rough in the new America and had had the Harley especially designed to withstand just about everything except a direct artillery hit. Heaving with all his strength, Stone pulled the Electraglide up out of the slime. It seemed to be stuck at first, but as he reached down inside him and pulled with everything in him, it came free of the mud with a loud sucking sound. It had turned off automatically—part of its design—but when he sat back in the driver's seat and hit the instant start button, the rhino-sized motorcycle started up again as if nothing had happened.

"Come on, pal," Stone shouted at the bull terrier, which stood to the side of the bike looking up at him as if getting back on the black machine was about the last thing in the world it had in mind. "Suit yourself," Stone said, starting slowly ahead. "But don't forget to write, okay." He turned his head forward and shifted into gear but had gone only a few yards when he felt the weight of the animal land squarely on the seat behind him. This time it sat up, rested its paws on the back of his shoulders and peered over his shoulder, keeping an intent eye on his driving maneuvers. Every now and then it would let out with a bark when they came to a puddle or got too close to a rock or cactus. For better or worse, Stone had created the world's first canine backseat driver.

CHAPTER
Four

S TONE HAD no idea how long they drove. In the midst of the black curtains of cold rain, he felt almost as if he were in a dream. It just seemed to go on forever and he fell into a kind of trance where all there was was keeping the bike upright and concentrating on the next few yards. But at last the rains seemed to diminish, and then, as if the heavenly water supply had run dry, stopped completely.

It was wet! As if the entire world had taken a bath. But the prairie had been through these things a million times before, and the members of the ecosystem that depended on water to give them life came out of their watery holes to gather the pickings. It was like the day after an immense and debauched party. Everything was wet, groundhogs were slicked back, their fur flat against their bodies so they looked like they'd just gotten some kind of punk hair styling, the bisons' thick hanging hides all matted together. But they started munching away at the droplet-covered vegetation as if nothing had happened.

Then he heard it. A low rumbling sound almost like a kettle drum far off, but seeming to come from every direction. Stone built up speed a little and when he felt comfortable that the bike wasn't going to take another tumble, increased until they were moving at about forty mph. But the dog was nervous, more so than when they had been in the thick of it. And by now Stone knew enough to trust the animal's instincts. It let out a high-pitched growl and half bit at his neck as if trying to tell him something. Stone stopped the bike and stood up on the seat.

With the engine turned off, he could hear the rumbling growing louder now and as he scanned the horizon and the base of the mountains about ten miles ahead of them, he saw what was causing it. And his face turned white as a sheet. For there was a wall coming at them from all sides. A tidal wave would be a better word. It was hard to judge just how far off it was, but even from some distance the wall had size, and that meant—he knew—that it was huge.

"Jesus Christ," he spat out angrily, looking up at the sky for a moment as if to say it was all a little too much. What the hell did God or nature or whoever ran things in this fucked up wet tub called earth have in store for him anyway. But nothing answered his curse, except the rising sound of the waterfall that coursed across the plain like a blob of living matter. The runoff from the rain, millions of gallons of it, cascading down the mountains. It had all melted together—drop joining drop, rivulet joining rivulet—until a monster had been created, a death-dealing tsunami.

He turned on the seat, almost slipping, and looked behind. But it was the same. The flood seemed to be coming from everywhere as if they were in the middle of the Red

Sea and Moses had already split the scene. Excaliber whined even louder and stared up at Stone, his oriental-shaped eyes growing wide as silver dollars on that pushed-in white face, as if to ask, you do know what to do, right?

"Let's get the fuck out of here," Stone blurted out and dropped back down hard onto the black leather. It hardly seemed possible that they could escape. There was nothing higher than a few rises that came up a yard or so above the flat prairie. But perhaps the greatest ability—and madness—of man is that he never gives up no matter how bad things look. They could hardly have looked worse than this.

Stone opened the Harley up, tearing across the wet plains straight for the mountain range ahead. He didn't even care if they fell over now; it hardly mattered. But the plan had a certain flaw because the faster they went, the closer the tidal wave came toward them. And it was growing in height now so that Stone could see the extent of the flood about to inundate them. The wall must have reached up a good twenty-five feet and seemed of even height across his entire line of view. The thunderous roar it let out as it rushed forward was quite disconcerting. There wasn't a chance in a million that they could ride through that.

He searched his brain frantically for options but came up with nothing. What would the major have done, Stone wondered, the pit of his stomach tight as a vise grip. The old man had seemed to have had an answer for everything. How the hell would he have gotten out of this one? He visualized his dead father's face, as if seeing his features clearly would somehow give him an answer. He remembered the major describing all the hardware of the Harley.

Wait! The old man had said something about a raft, a built-in job at the bottom of the bike. Stone had never gone

through the machine's entire inventory, other than the weaponry. There hadn't been a need. But now . . .

He screeched to a halt, nearly throwing Excaliber from the
seat and scanned the digital dashboard. There—EMERGENCY
RAFT—a small lever. But was he supposed to set the bike in a
certain position? How could . . . Fuck it, Stone decided suddenly as the tidal wave came to within a mile of them, bearing
down like something out of a biblical prophecy. There was no
time for heavy theoretical analysis. He took a deep breath and
flipped the lever to the RELEASE position.

There was a loud clicking sound from the bottom of the
Harley and a steel panel slid sideways. A bright orange raft
shot out below his feet and instantly began inflating from a
carbon dioxide canister built into it with a loud whooshing
sound. The raft spread out like a mound of Jello and filled
with the gas at a rapid rate. The sound seemed to frighten
Excaliber, who set to wailing again, deciding in his canine
brain that all things considered, this had been just about the
worst day of his life. As it filled, the edges of the raft spread
out in all directions so it quickly contained the entire Harley,
raising it up slightly. Within sixty seconds, they and the bike
were sitting in the center of the fully inflated flotation device
that spread out for about eight feet around them.

"I'll be damned," Stone muttered to himself, the traces of
a smile arching his face. The damned thing worked. He'd
have to check out *all* the features that the Harley possessed
—if he lived that long. For the wall of dark brown water
was almost upon them. It was impossibly large, foaming at
the top, cresting toward them as if reaching to suck the bike
and its occupants down to a watery grave. At the forefront of
the turning waves were trees, animals, cacti, all pulled along
like twigs as the flash flood ripped everything it encountered

into its dark guts. The pitbull sank back onto the seat and closed its eyes. Stone stared dead on into the rushing flood. If he was going to die he wanted to see it all. He said a silent prayer to unknown gods and waited. There was nothing to do but let it happen.

The tidal wave slammed into them with a deafening roar. Stone felt the impact of the water like a kick to the guts and then as if every cell in his body was being torn apart. His eyes shut involuntarily, not wanting to see the end even if he did. Then everything was spinning, the world flashing by around them like a top, and a tornado of liquid seemed to engulf them, taking them down. All Stone could see was water and then they went under. He took a deep breath and waited to die.

But he didn't. After a few seconds Stone opened his drenched lids and to his amazement they were floating along on the surface of the river of dark water, the lead waves already past them and heading on to see what else they could claim. The raft continued to turn at a dizzying rate and Stone wondered if he was going to puke. But after another minute, the raft slowed to a near crawl. It bobbed up and down like a cork on the now vast lake that filled the plains. Stone could see the unfortunate victims of the flood floating all around him. Carcasses of buffalo and deer, lizards and snakes, all twisting in the currents as if a burial ground of nature's creatures had been opened up. The bodies were already bloated, the tongues of the animals hanging out of their mouths, swollen and dark. Far overhead vultures began circling patiently. There was going to be some feasting done when the waters receded.

Stone sat back on the seat of the Harley, dead center of the thick plastic raft, which rode over the swells, drifting aimlessly about like a leaf in the ocean. Now that it was fully

sure it was actually going to survive the latest installment of
life with Martin Stone, the pitbull seemed to relax a little. It
jumped down from the seat and made a full circumference of
the raft, which extended several feet in each direction and
then rose at the edges like an immense rubber doughnut. The
Harley weighed half a ton plus with all its military hardware,
but though the center of the float was pushed in several feet
it didn't seem in any imminent danger of sinking. Excaliber
headed to the front of the thing and put both its paws up on
the raised round edge and stared forward like some sort of
living figurehead.

Something moved in the black rushing foam just ahead of
them and the pitbull barked loud and snapped at it. But it
was just a snake, a long black one, swimming frantically by.
It glanced at the raft with glowing red eyes, thinking for a
split second that it might be safety, but when it saw the
snapping jaws of the pitbull thought better of it and headed
past them, whipping through the water like an eel.

They floated for hours and if Stone was thankful for anything it was that the skies at least seemed to be clearing.
Another downpour would fill the raft—and that would be
that. He wasn't sure but it felt like the current, which originally had been in the direction of the water wall, now
seemed to have reversed and that they were starting to move
toward the mountains, still miles off. After an hour he was
sure of it. The current picked up and the raft with the huge
Harley bouncing in its center seemed to virtually motor forward, leaving a little trail of white bubbles behind them.

They rode this way, unable to do a thing about their direction except watch. The feeble sun that had finally broken
through sank behind them as if into the lake and the night
fell like a steel gate over the world. Still the raft surged
forward, now gaining speed as the mountains loomed larger,

lit on their snow-tipped peaks by a crescent moon hanging like a ghostly sickle in the sky. Then they were there, the slopes almost within reach, yet no way of reaching them. With the immense weight of the bike, paddling was absurd. There wasn't a fucking thing he could do to control the thing at all. Stone had never felt so helpless in his life and a kind of impotent anger filled his chest.

The raft was led between two towering peaks so it was now on a river about a hundred yards wide. And with the tremendous mass of water fed into it the going got rough again as the relatively smooth surface of the lake turned into white foaming rapids that rushed forward, guided by rock cliffs on each side. The flotation device began spinning and slamming up and down as the wave motion grew to three-, four-, then five-foot tongues of water. The Harley dug deep into the bottom of the float with each slap of water and Stone began wondering just how long it could take the strain. A few of the seams along the side started to unravel, the nylon stitching coming undone like the sides of an old pair of pants. But it held—for the moment.

As they shot down the river the sheer energy of moving water kept accelerating the raft until they were doing a good thirty mph. From time to time the orange float would bang against a boulder or the rough sides of the sheer rock banks and catapult them out again into the thick of it. It couldn't go on like this for much longer. Something was going to give and he knew it wasn't going to be the river.

Ahead Stone heard a crashing sound like the pounding of an immense fist into the earth. Then he saw the cloud of spray lit up by the moonlight sitting above the river about a half mile ahead, and just the traces of a rainbow spreading from shore to shore. He knew instantly what it was—a waterfall. If his face could go a deeper shade of pale, it did, as his heart began beating so fast he swore it would bust through his chest. He glanced up at the scimitar of a moon hanging in the sky as if it was about to cleave the world below it in two, and wondered just what the hell he had done, just which fucking god he had insulted—'cause somebody up there sure didn't like him.

CHAPTER
Five

THERE WAS nothing to do but die. Stone knew he had been living on borrowed time from the moment he left his father's bunker with his mother and sister April. His mother had died a horrible death at the hands of bikers and he was about to join her, wherever people went when their flesh turned cold. April at least was with Kennedy and somehow he knew the old man would take care of her—as long as he was alive anyway. It was the dog he felt worst about. He had warned the pitbull from the very start, had told him he was heading for trouble. But apparently the animal hadn't quite understood. Stone reached down and petted Excaliber on the head.

"Sorry, pal. You didn't deserve this," he said softly. The bull terrier looked up cheerfully and pressed his head against Stone's leg. Moisture formed at the edge of the eyes of the man who had stared down whole gangs of psychos without blinking. He thought insanely for a second of trying to heave the animal toward shore. But it was at least thirty yards through violent whirlpools of water. There was no way. It would be better for them both to go over the falls, which were growing to the roar of an artillery barrage just ahead. At least it would be quick.

Suddenly Stone thought he was hallucinating. A bright light appeared downriver, shooting rapidly toward them about fifty feet above the waterline. He thought for a moment that perhaps he was seeing some sort of optical illusion—the rays of the moon being bent by the aura of spray that hung over the lip of the falls. But the light grew closer and brighter until he could hardly look at it.

"You down there, can you hear me?" Stone stared up, his mouth hanging open. He squinted through the spray of the river and saw it—a helicopter, blades whirling in a solid blur as it hovered almost directly overhead.

"I said, can you hear me, man? There's no time left to fuck around. You've got seconds left to follow my instructions." The voice boomed out over some sort of loudspeaker mounted below the chopper's body with a shrill metallic static.

Stone cupped his hands around his mouth and screamed up, "I hear you. I hear you, for Christ's sake.

"We're going to drop a cable to you. Tie it to the most solid thing on the raft. And move fast!" Stone started to scream up again and then realized there was no way they could hear him through the roar of the falls. He nodded his head frantically up and down and held his arms wide, signaling he was ready. A side door opened on the chopper, which he could see was painted camouflage stripes and still had U.S. Army markings on the body. He didn't know what the hell was going on but he'd ask questions later if there was a later. A figure appeared at the door and dropped a

loop of cable straight down. Stone caught it and was almost
knocked to the ground as the inch-thick woven-steel cable
caught him in the face like a punch from a super heavyweight.

He almost blacked out from the blow and felt a sheet of
blood pour down his face. Stone shook his head to clear his
senses and then leaned down and clamped the eyehook
around the center of the handlebars.

"Are you secured?" The voice bellowed down again like
the voice of God. "I repeat, are you secured?" Stone stood
straight up and waved his arms up and down like a maniac,
signaling assent. "We're going to drag you to the shore.
Hang on, buddy." The man in the doorway waved a sign of
encouragement and Stone suddenly allowed himself a glim-
mer of hope that he was actually to get out of this damned
death river without being fish chow.

The chopper pulled away slowly to the left, letting the
cable take up the slack until it was taut. It wasn't a transport, more of a scout craft with a single machine gun
visible just inside the opening, and the chopper seemed to
struggle with the immense weight of the raft and the surging current of the river. It was as if the flood didn't want
to release its prey—not when they were so close to diges-
tion. But slowly, inch by inch, foot by foot, the helicopter
pulled against the flow and angled over to the rocky
shore. As they drew closer Stone could see other faces
and vehicles stopped along the top of the granite banks
about thirty feet up staring down at him, gesturing wildly
to one another as uniformed men hustled down the slope
and ran the few yards to the shore.

And then with a final burst of strength the chopper pulled
him out of the central currents and over into the stiller waters

along the edge. Hands reached out from everywhere and grabbed hold of the sides of the raft and dragged it up onto the bank.

"Jesus man, you are one of the luckiest son-of-a-bitches alive," the nearest face, a pimply-faced teenager in a brown uniform yelled to Stone above the screaming rotors of the chopper just above their heads.

"Tell me something I don't know." Stone grinned back, feeling like he could jump up and kiss every one of the blurred faces that surrounded him. "Who the hell are you guys?"

"Army," the youth shouted back. "U.S. Army—the New American Army to be exact. We were just heading toward—"

"I'll take charge here," a man coming down the steep cliff said as Stone stepped from the raft. Never had solid ground felt so wonderful. Excaliber seemed to have the same basic emotions as he jumped from the raft and barked wildly, running in happy circles.

"Are you injured?" the officer asked with the clipped quick tones of upper-echelon army brass. Stone had seen enough of them in his childhood. This one looked typical. Hard face that looked like it hadn't changed expression in a decade, tight white lips, concave cheeks giving him an almost cadaverous look. He stood at rigid attention in front of Stone who suddenly saw the patch on his shoulder—two M-16's crisscrossed over the American flag. And his rank—major. The soldier who had pulled Stone to safety, who had seemed friendly enough a minute before, now stood at rigid attention, eyes straight ahead, as did all the other troops, shoulders pulled back, chins tucked in, arms flat at their sides.

"Just my heart." Stone said, slapping his hand over his

chest. "I don't think it's going to ever slow down. I was just—"

"Name? Occupation?" The officer cut him off sharply. "We don't have time to exchange pleasantries."

"Name's Stone. Martin Stone," Stone answered, starting to take a dislike to the fellow, even though he owed his life to the crew. "As for my occupation, I didn't really know there were such things anymore. Mostly I've been just trying to keep my ass in one piece, and . . ." He was about to mention April and then thought better of it, remembering his father's words: "Never tell anyone more than you have to. You never know." You never know—that was the one fucking truth of life.

"We're ready up here," a voice yelled down and Stone looked up to the cliff some thirty feet above to see more men setting down a series of interconnecting ramps so as to form an instant roadway straight down the side of the granite slope.

"I'll question you more later," the officer said, looking Stone up and down as if he were examining some rather grotesque form of bug. Another cable was thrown down the ramp and two men attached it to the front of the Harley. The entire crew dragged the bike to the bottom of the steep ramp and Stone heard a motor start above them. With agonizing slowness the bike was dragged sideways right up the ramp as the uniformed soldiers, Stone and the pitbull made their way up the jagged sides of the slope. When he crawled onto the relatively flat surface that ran along the edge of the river Stone was if anything even more amazed than by anything else that had happened to him over the past twenty-four hours. For there was what looked like an entire army stopped on the dirt road: trucks, jeeps with field artillery hooked to the back of them and—his tired eyes could hardly

believe it—three tanks lined up one after another. Troops
were everywhere looking at him and the Harley being hauled
up to safety. There must have been over a hundred men.
Stone hadn't seen such an organized and heavily armed
force since he had emerged from the bunker. He hadn't even
thought that there were such units anymore.

"Load the motorcycle into the rear transport," the hollow-
cheeked officer yelled to the team that had hauled it up.
Stone walked quickly over to the man and tried to act as
friendly as he didn't feel.

"Look, thanks a lot and all that, but if you don't mind I'll
just take the bike and me and my dog will just be on our
way."

"I'm afraid that won't be possible at this moment," the
major snapped. "We're on a search-and-destroy operation
with strict orders to eliminate anyone we find. This area—
for your information—is a free-kill zone, meaning it's inhabited by murderers, cutthroats and cannibals, and we're sanitizing it."

"Free-kill zone? Sanitizing? What the hell are you talking
about?" Stone protested, his voice starting to rise as he momentarily forgot that he was outnumbered by a hundred to
one. "Who are you guys? Under what authority—"

"Later!" the officer barked. "You will have plenty of time
to discuss this all later." Stone was liking the guy less and
less every second. And the phrase "plenty of time" didn't
sound too promising. But he breathed out and tried to relax.
It wasn't the time or place to make any kind of move. The
major waved his hand and the ramp was pulled back up and
the bike wheeled back toward the transport that stood motionless about forty yards back.

"You'll have to come with us, sir," two of the uniformed
men said, suddenly standing on each side of Stone. They

were young but carried stern expressions and M-16's over their shoulders. "And please, keep control of your dog; we wouldn't want to have to shoot such a beautiful animal."

"Sure, pal, sure," Stone muttered, grabbing hold of Excaliber, who was starting to look a little pissed off at the whole scene. They weremarched back to the truck into which the bike was being wheeled up another ramp. The force was well equipped, Stone had to give them that. They seemed more like a unit of pre-war days than the typical ragged fighting man that he had encountered in the new America. He jumped up into the canvas-sided army truck, the pitbull leaping up beside him, followed quickly by the two guards, who apparently were going to keep a sharp eye on their rescued captive.

There was a sounding of horns up and down the line of vehicles and they started forward again, the transport he was in taking up the rear.

"Am I a prisoner or what?" Stone asked, smiling at the two young soldiers, who certainly didn't seem like killer types.

"Sorry, sir," the elder one, with a single stripe on his sleeve, said. "We're not allowed to discuss anything with you. Major Vargas will explain everything to you later."

"Well, who are you guys anyway? I mean, are you good guys or bad guys?" He knew the question was ridiculous, but he just couldn't tell.

"Sorry sir," the soldier said, staring past Stone as if he didn't even see him.

"Well, where are we going? Surely you can tell me that? I mean it's not like I'm heading out anywhere soon."

"Sorry sir," the corporal replied in the same monotone.

"You guys are really talkative. I haven't had such a stimulating conversation since my dog howled last night."

"Sorry sir," the soldier started to reply and then cut himself off as he realized what Stone had said. He looked away, embarrassed, but didn't utter another word.

Stone shut up. He sat on the hard wooden benches that ran along the inside of the truck and stared out the back. As the military convoy headed downriver they passed the waterfalls from which Stone had escaped by the hair on his balls. For the first time he saw what had awaited him and the pitbull. The water dropped a good hundred feet onto a maze of boulders below, where it exploded in a violent spray that rose into the air. Nothing could survive that drop. Nothing. He would have been crushed into something that would have made good soup starter and that's about it. And suddenly even his loquacious companions seemed better company than the waiting jaws of the fish, snakes and snapping turtles.

CHAPTER
Six

THEY HAD driven for about three hours in silence, Excaliber asleep at his feet, when Stone began feeling strange. Very strange. He thought at first it might be the bouncing, seesawing motion of the truck, for its suspension was clearly not in the greatest shape, but then waves of sharp pain swept through his hand, the one that had been bitten by the ear taker. Stone held it up to the dim light of dawn edging down through the open back of the truck and took in a sharp breath. The bite wound was swollen nearly an inch high and the entire back of his hand had started turning an extremely ugly dark purple. He pressed in on the flesh and it seemed to stay indented like a piece of rotten fruit, not springing back at all. Stone rolled up his sleeve to the elbow and again breathed in sharply. Bright red streaks ran side by side all the way up the inside of his forearm.

Suddenly he felt dizzy, the world spinning around him, as if he'd chugged a gallon of vodka. He tried to speak to the guards but heard nothing coming out, just his lips opening and closing and his mouth dry as sand, without a drop of spit. He stood up, feeling as if he were suddenly suffocating and lurched toward the two men, his legs feeling as if they were made of lead. The soldiers glanced up at him from out of their semi-dozes with startled eyes and swung their rifles around, clicking off the safetys.

"I-I," Stone could hear himself stuttering as he headed toward them an inch at a time like an old cripple hardly able to walk. Then it was as if all his blood drained from his body at one instant and poured out his feet and he felt so cold that he thought he would freeze to death in seconds. He saw the floor of the truck coming up at his face like a fist and felt a sharp blow as if he had been struck by a sledgehammer. Then everything went from black to gray and black again.

Somewhere were voices and faces that looked like demons, and hands, so many hands, touching him, moving him. Stone had the sense of motion, as if he were being carried, and broken images of the world—a mouth here, an eye there, peering down at him, just inches away—the sky flashing overhead, brilliant with pearl clouds dancing to his rapidly beating heart. But it was all confused, insane, as if he were watching a movie that had jumped its sprockets and the images were nonsensical, without real understanding. The worse thing was how far away he felt. Though his senses still perceived things, albeit in a distorted way, his mind felt like it was on another planet. He couldn't understand, comprehend anything. And somewhere inside of him, Martin Stone knew that death was very near, a dark brooding presence that circled around him, trying to pull him in, trying to draw him into its black fires.

Then he was in a tent or something and there were bright,

blinding lights burning into his eyes and needles piercing his skin. But he felt none of it, felt only a strange tingling sensation along his thigh and hip and up to his heart, like a little river of fire burning its way through his veins and arteries. Then there was darkness and terrible dreams.

He was in the ground. Under the soil. Sealed in below the hard unbearable pressing weight of the earth that covered him for many feet overhead. He knew he was dead. He couldn't quite remember how he had died, but nevertheless he was dead. And they had buried him. Except for one thing —he was still alive. Somehow. His mind knew where, who, what he was. There was no movement or warmth in his pale cold body but he knew that he was. Only he wasn't. He was dead. The living dead.

There were other dead things around him. He could sense their static but still-existing consciousness beating out in impotent fury. For they were all trapped here forever. This was Hell. Worse than Hell. He couldn't take it, to be trapped here, buried for ten billion years until the very universe came to an end. He had to live. Had to. Stone made the body come to life. He filled its cold fingers with warmth and made the leathery arms move. The corpse thing clawed at the dirt a grain at a time. His mouth and shriveled eyes were filled with the cold soil, crushing, grinding into him.

Still he clawed. Clawed and scratched with every bit of energy that lived in the soul of Martin Stone. And he created a hole in the dark dirt and pulled it down. His hand broke free above the ground and he could see a blue light that burned like a star. And his fingers clawed through until at last his skeletal shrunken head broke above the surface. The light filled his black eyes with glare so intense he was blinded. Something was roaring, a wind roaring through the worm-riddled holes that were his ears.

"Mister, mister. You awake or what? Your signs read that you're coming out of alpha rhythm into waking pattern. Mister, if you can hear me, open your eyes."

Suddenly Stone felt reattached to his own flesh. As if he wasn't a million miles away, but in it. And it was warm and he could taste the oxygen filling his lungs like the sweetest perfume. He was alive. He opened his eyes and looked up into a pair of crystal-blue eyes with a face of an angel built around them. The face smiled and bent so close Stone could smell the presence of her female flesh.

"Where am I? What's happened to me? Last thing I remember I was in the truck." Stone sat up, suddenly alarmed. "My dog, where—"

"Relax," the young blonde woman said, and Stone noticed that her eyes weren't one color but seemed to ripple from blue to green to gray like a rainbow. She pushed him back down with a soft hand. "Your dog's fine, you're in the NAA Hospital in Grand Junction, Colorado. As to what happened. You almost died, mister. Came this close," she said, holding her fingers just a fraction of an inch apart. "That bite you got on your hand—from whatever romantic entanglement you were involved in—had set in a number of different infections. But basically you had blood poisoning. The germs spread up the veins and the arteries, heading toward your heart. The doctor said, two or three more hours —and forget it. We pumped so much antibiotics, penicillin and every other goddamned thing we could find in this place into your blood we probably drowned whatever what was hungry in there."

"I see," Stone said, smiling slightly through a not unpleasant haze. He liked the way she cursed, the way she moved, everything about her. If there was a reason to live, it was standing right in front of him.

"You're lucky, mister. Damned lucky. Fifty years ago, you would have been dead. But even with every drug known to man shot into you you've still been in pretty much of a coma for about two-and-a-half days. We didn't know if you were going to make it or not. But about six this morning your brain activity increased markedly and—"

"How do you know so much about my brain activity?" Stone asked with a grin.

"We've got all kinds of heavy duty medical equipment here. Two operating rooms, and all this gear too." She pointed across the room and Stone's eyes followed to see computers, readout graphs, beeping lines that squiggled and wavered like electronic snakes.

"What is *all this* anyway?" Stone asked, motioning with his head in a circle to sort of include everything. "What is the NAA. I don't know anything about the whole setup as I wasn't given a bit of information from the moment I was rescued."

"You're lucky they didn't kill you," the woman said. Stone noticed for the first time she was wearing a nurse's uniform, starched and white and tight-fitting in all the right places. He looked her up and down appreciatively. "They sometimes make sweeps of certain areas where there's been a lot of trouble and just level everything. The New American Army, that's who we are. You're at the main headquarters of the NAA here in Grand Junction, although there are several other outposts that have been established, I'm not sure where. They don't tell us a lot about what's going on."

"But what is it that you do exactly?" Stone asked. "I mean, army for who? For what?"

"For ridding America of the bandits and murderers and warlords who control everything. For pulling the U.S. back from the very edge of a barbarism that will make the Dark Ages seem like an afternoon brunch. You've seen what it's like out there. We're going to reestablish the United States, unite her again, rid her of the lice and vermin who are out there." Stone had a strange sensation as he listened to her. For the words were something he agreed with wholeheartedly, but the way she said them—her eyes wide and almost blank, her voice rising—it was almost as if she were in some kind of stupor, or trance.

"How many are there of you? Who runs the show? I noticed, before I passed out, that everyone had ranks like the old army."

"There must be about three hundred at this camp," she said, adjusting his pillow as he began feeling very tired again. "More at other places. General Patton runs everything. He is the Supreme Commander. He was able to keep control of a small army unit that was in charge of a munitions depot. After America collapsed he came out and has been fighting his way around this part of the country, gathering men. Fighting the enemy wherever he exists. The general is a brilliant man. You can see for yourself." She moved her hands around the antiseptically clean recovery room. "This hospital here, as primitive as it might be compared to the old days, is probably one of the most modern and well equipped in the country right now. The general is not just a master of strategy, but of organization, of gathering and distributing military supplies to all his units. Of keeping things working, and keeping men under control. All of us are volunteers, and proud to serve in the NAA."

"What's your name?" Stone asked suddenly, feeling more tired by the second and wanting to know who she was so he could call up her memory in his sleep, so he could dream of her to get strength.

"I'm Nurse Williamson," she said, smiling a little nervously and looking down. "And you, we couldn't find any ID on you anywhere?"

"Didn't see the point, to tell you the truth, Nurse Williamson," Stone said, liking the way the syllables of her name slid off his tongue like velvet. "I mean there's not too many traffic cops giving out tickets anymore. My name's Stone, Martin Stone," he answered and suddenly his lips would hardly move.

"Martin, that's a nice name," he barely heard her whisper. Then she was injecting him with something and he felt himself falling into a pit again. But this time a pit of sleep—not of death.

CHAPTER
Seven

THE NEXT time he woke up, Stone thought perhaps he might actually make it. His body felt fully his again. It was as if he had reasserted, by sheer force of will, his being into all of his cells. Everything still hurt like a motherfucker. He felt like he had been on the biggest drunk of his life. He lifted his hand and looked at it. It was black and blue, with an almost luminous sheen to it as if the skin had been pressed very tight. It must have swollen up tremendously, but now it was almost flat again, just felt like it had been under a ten-ton press for a year or two. He looked up and down his arms but the red streaks were all gone. He remembered for a second his corpse dream—had it been real? He prayed not. If that was what death really was...he shuddered. Well, it proved one thing, Stone thought. He had always pretended, at least to himself, that he didn't give a shit whether he lived or died. But now that he had seen death, he wanted to live. He did give a shit. He would fight to his last sputtering breath not to go.

Stone took a deep breath, realizing it was time to get his life in gear again—if not actually zooming, at least hobbling along. He sat up, spun around in the bed and stood up. The white walls of the room undulated around him as if he were in a carnival funhouse, but within seconds his head cleared and he started toward the door. He felt a sudden pain in his right arm and stopped short.

"Shit," he cursed as he saw that he had forgotten about the IV unit pumping white liquid into the vein inside his elbow. He reached over and closing his eyes pulled the needle out, letting it fall and dangle at the end of the rubber feed tube. It hurt. He glanced around and grabbed a swab of cotton from a desk next to the bed and a roll of tape and quickly and crudely wrapped the lightly bleeding hole up. He had to get moving. He started across the floor.

"Ah, Mr. Martin Stone," a female said, opening the buffed aluminum door. "I see you're up and about and"— her eyes ran quickly up and down his body—"I presume looking for your clothes." Stone glanced down suddenly and realized he was stark naked. He felt suddenly embarrassed, vulnerable, his feet on the cold floor, in front of her. Nurse Williamson didn't pull her eyes away, but just kept staring at him, just below his belly button. A thin smile jogged back and forth across her mouth.

"Not bad," she said, stopping in her tracks and crossing her arms. "Not bad at all."

"Come on, where are they?" Stone asked. "I'll have a relapse and die for sure if you don't tell me where my clothes are."

She went to a six-foot aluminum cabinet and opened the

door. "Here, you can wear these for now—an NAA uniform, roughly your size. Dress and I'll show you around." She walked back to the door, stopped and turned again, her eyes focusing on him again.

"Well," Stone asked, starting across the floor to the cabinet, feeling like an idiot.

"Well what," Nurse Williamson asked, flipping her shoulder-length hair around one shoulder and looking at him hard. Her body was beautiful. There was no other way to describe it. Through the nurse's gear he could see the round curve of her hips, the melon breasts standing fully out, pressing against the white cotton as if they wanted to burst free. Now, if she had been undressed too, it would have been a different matter.

"Well—I want to dress for Christ's sake, lady. I know it's the army and all that, but a man still has his sense of privacy."

"I'm a nurse, sweetie," she said, smiling at him. "Seen lots of men's bodies. Naked, dead, sliced up into so many pieces. I've seen it all, believe me, you get to know every part of a man. You know what I mean?" Stone gulped and dressed quickly. The woman had a way with words that made him feel his family jewels were about to be scalpeled away.

"Come on," she said when he was ready. "It's just dinner time. We'll walk over to the commissary and you can see the camp along the way." She led him along a hallway and then down a flight of stairs. The hospital wasn't high tech, but it was clean, well scrubbed, light bulbs in place, all of them actually functioning. Stone hadn't seen anything this together since he'd been out of the bunker. It gave him a sudden stirring of hope in his guts. It almost hurt—hope. He had pushed it all down. The new America seemed . . . like hell, from what he'd seen so far. He had been fighting through a sea of blood from the moment he'd emerged after five years of living hidden inside a mountain fallout shelter. And the people he'd seen had been pretty fucking bad. These were the first who . . . seemed even vaguely to be on the side of life. Maybe things could be put together again. Maybe Humpty Dumpty could be glued and stitched up and placed back up on the wall. Maybe.

"My dog," Stone suddenly said loudly, feeling an instant wave of guilt for not having thought of it before. "Where is—"

"He's fine. I promise you. He knew we were helping you. He was trying to help you when you went down—licking your face, trying to lift you by pulling your collar up, to get you moving again. The guards reported they had a problem with him at first. But once he saw that he couldn't do anything and that they had good intentions, he let them treat you. He was taken to a special pound we have; they're handling him well, I swear."

"You don't understand; he doesn't get along with other dogs. He's a real scrapper. I've seen him—"

"There are other pitbulls here, Mr. Stone," she said with a smile as they reached the ground floor and walked along another antiseptic hall. "General Patton III breeds pitbulls here—as his namesake did. The dog handlers have much experience in handling the animal."

"But—but," Stone stuttered, somehow not imagining the animal allowing itself to be caged and fed army gruel—and God only knew what all.

"After dinner, I'll take you there. First thing."

Stone hesitated. He should see it immediately. But the dog would have eaten first before coming to save him. And he was starving.

"After dinner," Stone agreed, walking a little faster as his stomach began growling from even the thought of food. It had probably been days and days since he'd eaten anything beyond the muck they had been feeding into his veins.

She led him past a guard who sat on duty at the front door. The soldier, a private, jumped to quick attention as he saw her coming. He was young, in his late teens or early twenties, with an almost gawkish look about him. He gave the NAA salute—fist about three inches in front of the nose, arm stretched out sideways, parallel to the ground.

"He's okay," she said, nodding at Stone, who walked just beside her. "He's been cleared for minimum supervision. He'll be in my custody."

"Yes sir, Lieutenant," the man said, dropping the salute.

"At ease, Corporal," Nurse Williamson said. She led Stone out the door and into the sunlight. It was so bright it instantly made his eyes tear up and he had to stop for a second.

"Come on now, I can't carry you," she said, looking at him impatiently.

"Look Ms. Nurse," Stone said coolly. "I was shooting craps with the grim reaper just twenty minutes ago; it makes a guy a little dizzy. You should try it sometimes."

"Sorry," she answered, giving him a real smile for the first time, which quickly froze as she turned away. "Come on, let's move it." They walked down a concrete pathway and out onto a main road, asphalt, very smooth and black as if recently put down, and turned to the right. The camp was laid out logically and simply—all square buildings with wide thoroughfares between them. There were barracks to one side, each about sixty feet long by twenty feet high, over fifty of them. A cleared field was filled with vehicles —maybe forty jeeps, two dozen plus half-track type vehicles covered with thick steel armor, on high reinforced super wheels—the things looked lethal—and more of the tanks he had seen the night they rescued him, nearly twenty of them, all the same model—the Bradley III if his memory served him right. Dead center of the wide parking area stood rows of gasoline tanks, huge thirty-foot steel cylinders filled with the valuable motor fuel, worth more than gold these days. On the other side of the main thoroughfare, a number of two-story warehouses for arms and munitions that looked, by the wooden crates standing outside some of them waiting to be loaded, filled to capacity.

Stone was impressed. Very impressed. This General Patton, or whoever the hell he was, had gathered a substantial strike force. Given enough time, enough energy, he might well somehow gain control of the country. Although how he could weave together the disparate criminal and even savage elements that the new United States had become was beyond him.

Stone noticed as they walked that the entire encampment was surrounded by a fifteen-foot-high fence of barbed wire crowned link fence. And from the electrical equipment that stood nearby, it was probably able to electrocute, even kill those who touched it. Machine-gun towers stood at the four corners of the camp and in the center of each gated wall. From here they commanded a view of cleared field around the fort that extended hundreds of yards. The place seemed invulnerable.

Nurse Williamson pushed through a pair of swinging doors and they entered into a boisterous, soldier-filled cafeteria lined with fifty long tables, every one of them filled to the brim. Stone almost reeled back for a second at the sudden encountering of so much energy. But no one really paid much attention to them—too busy cramming bowls of steaming food and loaves of bread into their mouths. She led him up along one side and to a set of trays. Stone walked slowly along the bowls of food, huge canisters four feet high with ladles sitting around them.

"Take as much as you want," Nurse Williamson said, pointing down. "We believe in feeding people here. General Patton believes that a filled stomach is a loyal stomach."

"He's damned right about that. I've seen people die over a piece of bread," he answered, loading up with what looked like beef stew with carrots and onions. Food like people used to eat. "Jesus, this is incredible," Stone said with a smile on his face. He almost felt like a kid. Like he wanted to pile his plate high with everything. Take two plates, a whole loaf of bread. But he contained himself and merely filled the plate to overflow.

"Here, sit here," Williamson said, leading him to a table that was obviously reserved for officers, roped off to one side, near some windows. There were about a dozen higher ranks sitting around the table chewing away and they looked up at Stone and the nurse. They took two empty places along one side. Some of the officers, captains, colonels, a few majors, didn't look too pleased at his joining them. But they didn't say anything.

"Hey, ain't you the fellow they picked up just before the falls?" one of the officers directly across from Stone asked.

"Yeah, I'm the fool who ended up heading for Niagara Falls without a barrel." Stone grinned back sheepishly. "And to every man in this unit I'd like to give my thanks," Stone said, looking quickly around the table. "I really mean it. And the medical treatment I received when you all could have let me die. I haven't seen this level of civilization anywhere—to say the least." He took a bite of the pungent stew and felt his stomach growl. It tasted so good. Sending his mind back to better days when his mother had cooked thick stew on a winter's night. Days gone forever.

"Well thanks, mister," one of the hardfaced colonels sitting next to him said. The rest seemed to have relaxed a little at Stone's expression of gratitude. All men like to be complimented. "And welcome to the New American Army if anyone hasn't welcomed you yet. You look like you'll be a great recruit—once you can move your hand again." They all laughed. "I heard you near got yourself bitten to death." The colonel grinned. "A heroic way to go."

"Recruit?" Stone asked between bites. "I didn't know I'd volunteered."

"Oh, all able-bodied men are strongly suggested to join the NAA. Why, it's an honor to serve under General Patton III. Only one man in five can even meet the standards he's set. Besides, I would think you'd want to join up with the only official U.S. force trying to establish law and order in America. Help us create a future. If you've been out there, you've surely seen what it's like."

"Maybe he's on the wrong side," a colonel said, a reddish scar running along the side of his face from ear to chin. He stared at Stone like he wouldn't have minded shooting him dead on the spot. "I mean, he *is* a biker. And from what I've seen, bikers are scum. Why, we've already taken out nearly a hundred of the bastards."

The others stared at Stone to see how he would respond to the insult.

"Just because I ride a motorcycle," Stone answered, letting his fork drop to the side of his bowl, "doesn't mean I'm a murderer. It seems a little absurd to judge a man by his mode of transportation." Several of the faces grinned. They weren't all against him. "As to what side I'm on. That's hard to say. I'm still not sure exactly what side all of you are supposed to represent. So it's a little hard to judge myself, as you apparently find it so easy to do."

"The amount of armaments you carry on that motorcycle," the scar-faced colonel went on, spitting out every word like they were curses, "make it appear that you're capable of wreaking heavy destruction. Just what have you been using them for?"

Stone didn't like the third degree, but he wasn't in a position to do what he felt like, which was to slam a fist into the son-of-a-bitch's face. "Look mister," he said, talking slow and cold, "I've just been trying to survive, that's all. I've been battling the same assholes that you have. Just traveling around this part of the country is like being in a full-scale war. What would you have me do—carry a little white flag and give out flowers to everyone who tries to kill me?"

The colonel's face flushed and the jagged scar on his face seemed to turn three shades redder, virtually throbbing like a thing alive. His mouth twitched a few times and then he rose, addressing the rest of the table.

"Well, you can all stay here if you want, but as for myself I won't eat with scum like this. This biker"—he said the word with a most insulting inflection—"has no place sitting at a table with honorable men, or even being inside our walls. He sullies the very honor of our army." With that he threw his napkin to the table with a dramatic flourish and walked quickly away. Stone stared after him, his own heart beating fast. It might not have been the greatest thing after all to have been rescued by these guys.

"Sorry about that," the major across from him spoke up. "Colonel Matheson is a little quick to jump to conclusions.

My own philosophy is, don't judge a man until you've seen him on the battlefield." He looked at Stone expectantly.

"Right," Stone answered, lapping up his food with quick angry strokes. "Nor the character of a man by the number of wheels beneath his ass."

CHAPTER
Eight

"MATHESON'S NOT really a bad sort," the major who seemed somewhat friendly said. "He's with I&CE, Intelligence and Counter-Espionage, so he's always on the alert for saboteurs and troublemakers. Sees them coming out of the woodwork sometimes. But it's his job, that's all."

"I'm surprised that anyone would even attempt to mess around in here," Stone said, sopping up the last of his gravy with a thick slice of excellent homebaked rye bread. "You guys look like you're ready for World War IV."

"Oh, you'd be surprised," the major replied. "There's a lot of criminal groups who've tried to find out what we're doing in here—and stop it. We've had three infiltrators in the last six months. They didn't last very long. As I'm sure you'll find out, our security system is quite foolproof."

"I look forward to it," Stone said, not quite enjoying the

fact that all twelve pairs of vacuum eyes were still glued on him.

"Tell me Mr.—uh—" one of the colonels asked, an old hawk-faced fellow with all kinds of medals and insignias adorning his uniform on chest and shoulders.

"Stone, Martin Stone," he answered suddenly, wishing he had a calling card to hand out to all the stiff bastards with their razor-pressed uniforms, their chests covered with bright trinkets. Something lewd perhaps—one of those 3D women whose clothes came off as you turned her holographic image. Something about their stern military demeanor made him want to shock them, shake them up, see their tight white faces turn red. Maybe because they reminded him of his father, Major Clayton, whom Stone had fought will-to-will against from the time he was seven years old and began resisting the major's plans to mold him into a mirror image of the old man.

"Yes—Mr. Stone—how exactly did you end up on a Harley Davidson in a raft floating down the Green River about to go over Whitewater Falls?"

"You really want to know?" Stone asked with a kind of smirk as he looked quickly around the table. Their curiosity aroused, Stone decided to let them have it.

"Well, let's go back about five years," he said, taking a deep breath. "It all began when my father, Major Clayton R. Stone, took me and the rest of the family into a bombproof shelter he had built in a northern section of Estes National Park in Northern Colorado." Stone told them the whole damned story, whether they wanted to sit there or not. From the five years inside the mountain fortress to his father's death by heart attack and the subsequent leaving of the hideaway to see just what the hell was out there. He told them of the family being attacked by bikers—of his mother's rape and mutilation, Stone's being left to die, wounded in a hundred places, and his last-second reprieve when he was rescued by a tribe of nearby Ute Indians. And then how he had set out to find April, his sister. He told them of the bikers he'd faced and killed, of the Dwarf, that hideous quadriplegic killer, the Mafia crime lords he'd taken on, the firestorm of Denver, the destruction of the Last Resort. Martin Stone sat there, looked them all right in the eyes and told them every wretched second of the hell he'd been through.

"And that's how I ended up heading toward the goddamned waterfall," Stone finally finished his rap. Every face was glued to him, every set of eyes riveted to his. The tale of blood had gone on over half an hour, but not one had left, or even taken another bite of their now cold food.

"Either you're the biggest goddamned liar who ever walked the face of this planet," the colonel who had asked him to speak said from across the plate and tray-covered table, "or you're one tough, brave son-of-a-bitch. In either case let me shake your hand."

He stood up and reached across the table with a big hand and took Stone's firmly. "I'm Colonel Edgely, they call me the Hawk, though never to my face, because I'm in charge of supplies and I watch them like one. But I'm a fair and honest man. And I think you're one too. Besides, you've got the blood in you. Military blood. Your father, from what you say, was a fine fighting man. You've got to carry on his line. You've come to the right damned place. I'll tell you that. There's plenty of fighting to be done here."

Colonel Edgely sat back down with a thump as his large frame banged down onto the wooden chair. "Here, let me introduce you," he said, pointing with his right hand around the table. "This is Major Terkins, in charge of training—I expect you might be seeing a lot of him. And here—Lieutenant Connors, our communications coordinator, and this—" The colonel went all the way around the table, though Stone had forgotten the first name by the time they reached the second man. He nodded to each one, trying to force some sort of thin smile. He'd been out in the hell lands so long—where the faces were about as friendly as the muzzle of a loaded .45 and a smile could get you killed—that Stone had almost forgotten how to bend the mouth upwards at both ends into something approximating the proper expression. Now was as good a time as any to start practicing if he was going to work his way back into "polite" society. Some of them looked vaguely friendly, others not. None of them returned the smile. But he wasn't going to worry about that. Since most of the folks he'd met recently had been trying to kill him, a few nasty looks felt like hugs and kisses.

"But tell me," Stone asked curiously, when the intros had been completed. "What kind of military operations do you men carry out? I mean, aside from looking like the D-Day invasion force."

"We've been fighting, son, fighting the bikers, the warlords and the crime organizations who've divided America up into a goddamned bloody pie, that's what," Colonel Edgely said, leaning forward and slapping his fist on the top of the table so that half the dishes and silverware did a little quick dance in the air and then slammed down again. "For two years now, the Third Army under General Patton III has been out kicking ass, trying to get things sorted out. At the beginning there were just a hundred of us—all that was left of army training exercises in the Utah mountains. But after the Third World Alliance and the European forces shut things down, and the president fled the capital, we all just stayed out there.

"It was tough at first, but General Patton III isn't like other men. He's . . . a military genius; he kept it all together, gathered supplies and slowly built us up into what we are today—over a thousand men spread over three different states. Someday history will judge him to be one of the greatest generals of all time, a man whose name will be spoken in the same ranks of Napoleon, Caesar and his illustrious namesake General Patton, who kicked Nazi ass all the way back to the Berlin bunker." Col. Edgely's face grew redder and his eyes blinked open and closed like windshield wipers, so enthralled did he become with his own description. Stone couldn't help but be impressed. The colonel, all of them, seemed to almost worship this general, ready to do anything for him.

"Why, just this year, we've made three major search-and-destroy sweeps, taken out over five hundred mountain bandits, thugs, cannibals and all the other indefinable slime that's out there. Slowly, slowly we're clearing the way. And now General Patton is planning his boldest move of all—to wipe out the entire Mafia and Guardian of Hell operation in Colorado and Utah, to attack them at—"

"Colonel Edgely," Major Townsend, whom Stone somehow remembered from the introductions to be in charge of strategic planning, directly under the general, spoke up sharply. "May I remind you that what you are saying is top security information, and should not even be spoken of outside of the War Room!"

Edgely looked like he was going to blow a gasket for a second and then thought better of it and let the air slide out between his teeth with a low whistling screech. "Of course, of course, you're right, I forgot myself in the enthusiasm of the moment." Edgely said, trying to look as if he wasn't pissed off by the attack from a lower rank.

"It's okay," Stone said, looking at the fat, doughlike face of the protesting major, his cheeks like a squirrel's filled with nuts for the winter. "I'm not a spy, saboteur or a cannibal, I can promise you that. Setting yourself to go over one-hundred-foot waterfalls with about two seconds to spare is not exactly the ideal mode of operation for a well-trained spy. Or so I would imagine."

"Well, suffice it to say," Colonel Edgely coughed, daring anyone else to say a word, "that under General Patton the New American Army will reclaim the U.S.A., return her to her days of pride and glory. We are the wave of the future, Martin Stone. We will win, make no mistake about it. We've got the equipment, and the know-how to do it. We are all strong, patriotic men, willing to give the rest of our lives to the task."

He looked around the table with a smirk as the hard faces of the hardest of men stared back. "I don't care what any of these old bastards think," Edgely said, knowing that his high rank and regard by General Patton (with whom Edgely had served all the way back to Vietnam) gave him a privileged status—a nearly invulnerable position—at least from those back stabbers trying to rise from the below.

"You could join with us," he said with an almost religious fervor, as he stared directly into Martin's eyes with his own glowing orbs. "Rise with us as we fight the good fight. You're a smart lad, and tough—if your story is the truth. You could rise to the top. All of us are old here. I'm seventy-eight, Colonel Barrow is in his late sixties. Most of us have been around too long, though none of the others here would admit it." The rest of the officers looked down angrily. "We need fresh blood. Rather than keeping out men like you, we should encourage you to enter our ranks. You could well be the general of tomorrow, a senator of the new America. Whatever you want could be in your grasp. In ten years we'll control America. And those men who know what they're doing, men who can really think rather than just follow orders. Those men will rule, Stone, will create the new world. The question is: could you be one? Do you have what it really takes or are you just talking?"

"I'm not sure if I want—" Stone began to protest, when waiters suddenly appeared from everywhere, handing out large steins.

"Ah, beer time," Colonel Edgely exclaimed, grabbing the froth-topped stein and holding it to his lips. "Drink up, Stone, it's our own—brewed right here in one of the warehouses. Best damned beer in the West. Ain't like the cow piss you buy at some of these backwater taverns."

Stone took his and gulped down a few swallows. It was good. With a home-brewed sour taste that was not at all unpleasant. After a few minutes some of the soldiers seated around the hall began singing. Patriotic songs. Songs of America's past, and of her glorious future. They stood and swung their steins and sang their hearts out.

"I think I'd better leave," Stone said after about ten minutes, leaning over toward Nurse Williamson. The beer and the food had hit his still recovering nervous system like a ton of bricks. And he just wanted to get out into the cool night air. She rose and they walked down a side aisle past the singing, red-cheeked troops of the NAA. Stone couldn't help but notice how young most of the men seemed. Hardly out of their teens, many of them. But they seemed decent enough people. Stone felt moved by the proceedings in spite of himself. He had always had a sharp distrust of the military, growing up under his father's semi-tyrannical reign, yet these people all seemed basically good. It was hard for him not to be cynical about humanity after all that he'd seen. But if anyone really gave a shit, these guys had his vote for most likely candidates so far. Yet he felt oddly ill at ease about something. And he hadn't the slightest idea what it was.

"So how'd you like our staff, Mr. Stone?" Nurse Williamson asked as they walked out into cricket-cracked silence, as a cold mountain breeze raced down the central street and hit them both in the faces like ice water. Stone liked it, as it somehow woke him up from a stupor he had been starting to fall into. She shivered and edged subconsciously a little closer to him.

"They seemed well-intentioned enough," he replied, and then looked over at her with a quizzical expression. "Tell me, what exactly do *you* get out of all this. I mean, aside from the opportunity to help kill America's enemies and all that?"

"I get a place, Mr. Stone," she said without breaking stride, without looking up. "I was . . . alone, to say the least. My mother and father were killed in a not very pleasant fashion which I won't go into right now." Her eyes began tearing up slightly, Stone could see from the little slivers of reflected moonlight that shimmered across her cheek. "And I was on my own. I hid mostly during the day in a cave I found and came out at night armed with a butcher knife to rummage for food. I was attacked numerous times—barely survived. To tell you the truth, I was pretty much thinking of ending it all, of killing myself, and was just trying to think of a relatively painless way to do it—I could never stab myself. And then scouts from the NAA showed up. They could have killed me. I attacked two of them with the knife, thinking they were going to rape me again. But they disarmed me and after seeing I wasn't a mental case or sick from radiation poisoning they brought me back to their camp. I've been here ever since—about eighteen months now. And I won't ever go back out there—on my own. Not until it's all changed. I can sleep in here. Without having nightmares. Can walk around without being half crouched over, holding a blade in my hand. It's a life, Mr. Stone, a real life, where I have a roof over my head and food in my stomach and most of all where I have a purpose."

"I see," Stone said softly. They all spoke so highly of the New American Army. Everything was wonderful. He just wished even one person would be vaguely critical. *He* was just a troublemaker—that was his problem.

"Excaliber!" Stone suddenly exclaimed, stopping in his tracks. "I've got to—"

"Where do you think we're heading right now," she answered, taking a left turn as they approached an intersection. Stone could hear the barking from a block away. The unmistakable sounds of a dog pound and, as they grew closer, the thick pungent smells of animals, a shitload of them. They entered one of the wide two-story warehouses that seemed to be the main building design for the entire camp and Stone stared around in amazement. The place was filled from top to bottom with cages, all loaded with dogs of one kind or another. Everything from Dobermans to Newfoundlands to German shepherds—most of them settling back down to sleep after some disturbance had riled the place up. The two handlers on duty were walking up and down the pens, calming them down.

"Why so many dogs?" Stone asked Williamson as she led him down the middle of the place, which with its hundred-by-hundred-foot space filled to the rafters with dogs smelled and felt more like a zoo than an army storage depot.

"General Patton is a dog lover and breeder," she answered, glancing over nervously as they passed an immense Doberman that stared unflinching back at them. "He's concerned that a number of the purebred species will die out or become genetically damaged by radiation so as to produce only mutant and weakened offspring. These animals represent a relatively clean germ pool from which to restock. His dream is that after the country is restored to law and order these dogs will be reintroduced back into the population."

"Sort of a Noah's Ark of canines?" Stone said with a grin.

"Exactly." She laughed. "And I think yours must be over here somewhere." They walked into a section that was filled with pitbulls, both American and English. They were a beautiful lot and Stone let out with a low whistle. To see so many of the breed in one place was quite a sight—their black and brown and white and mixed coats shining like lions' manes. The handlers clearly took excellent care of their charges. It was evident in all the animals' bright eyes and brushed coats.

Suddenly Stone saw it—he knew the dog instantly—and rushed over to the six by six by six pen in which Excaliber was locked. It made something sink in the pit of his stomach to see the animal caged up. When he had originally found it the dog was locked in a Plexiglas prison along with a number of other animals at a biker bar.

"How you doing, boy?" Stone asked, kneeling down. Excaliber rose from a piece of cardboard in a corner of the pen and ambled over to Stone. He barked softly in recognition and licked at Stone through the mesh enclosure, his long wet tongue slopping over everything in sight. "You all right. They been treating you all right?" Stone looked around and saw a bowl filled with water and next to it what looked like ground up meat of some kind. If the pitbull was getting fresh meat, he was doing a hell of a lot better than he had done under Stone, who had been more likely to feed him cookies and beer than the nutrients that a growing dog needed.

Stone wanted the animal to be unhappy. To bark and whine and beg to come back with master. But after a mildly affectionate greeting, it turned, went back to the food bowl and began lapping up some of the red meat inside. It seemed perfectly content with the setup.

"Ingrate," Stone muttered under his breath.

"What was that?" Nurse Williamson asked, standing next to him.

"Nothing, just insulting my dog for not being more loyal," Stone said as he stood up. Well, if the damned dog was so happy in there it could just stay inside another night, Stone thought with disgust. He waved good-bye with a little salute.

"Adios, amigo—happy eating," Stone said. Excaliber glanced over with one cocked eye but didn't lift his head from the bowl, unwilling to miss one second of life's most wonderful experience.

CHAPTER
Nine

"YOU DON'T seem to like the fact that your dog seems none the worse for wear," Nurse Williamson commented as they headed back out to the front of the landbound animal ark.

"That's correct," Stone said. "In general, I think it's wonderful what General Patton is doing to preserve these species. Someday the world will thank him. But I've always resisted military training—wearing a uniform, loud 'yessir's' and all that. I spent the first twenty or so years of my life fighting against that approach to things with everything inside me. So when I see my dog seem to go under the influence so easily, I guess I don't like it. I want him to be a square cog in a round hole, to be anti-rules and regulations like his master . . . and I especially don't like seeing him happy inside a cage. It's not a place for anything, let alone a fighting dog with the intelligence and energy that his species has."

Stone stopped, suddenly catching with his peripheral vision two shapes coming quickly out of the shadows from behind the warehouse. Instinctively he raised both hands for combat before he saw their uniforms. Then he let his clenched fists loosen and drop to his side with a self-disgusted laugh.

"I see what you mean about not having to defend yourself all the time," Stone said, looking at Williamson. "I'm ready to fight anything that moves—trees, clouds, you name it. I think my paranoia level has risen through the danger mark since I've been out there."

"Mr. Stone?" one of the soldiers asked, and Stone noticed that aside from being large fellows with a certain Cro-Magnon look each of them had a somewhat ominous emblem on their lapel—a golden eagle carrying a skull in its claws.

"They're Internal Security, I.S.," she said to Stone, sensing his apprehension.

"We'd like to have a brief talk with you, Stone," one of them said as they parked themselves on each side of him and crossed their oak tree arms in a don't-even-try-to-run-one-inch kind of relaxed demeanor. "It will just take a few minutes. Colonel Spears would like to go over a few things with you."

"Sure," Stone said, burping. "Will there be any dessert?"

"Dessert, sure," the other two-forty-pound plus trooper grunted with a little laugh.

"It will be okay," Nurse Williamson said, holding onto his arm and starting forward. "I'll come with you and then I've got to get you back to the ward; you shouldn't even really be out right now. He's a sick man," she said, looking up at the I.S. men. "I'm supposed to give him another set of antibiotic shots and treat his wound."

"You go," the higher-ranked one said, pulling her arm

free of Stone's and steering her toward the hospital at the other end of the encampment. "He'll be there in time to get his shots. He's a big boy, and he can handle himself."

"Get the needles ready," Stone said to her as he walked off between the two uniformed gorillas. "Especially black cherry, that's my favorite flavor." They led him down one of the side streets to a warehouse painted black—this one with machine-gun emplacements on each side of the roof, thirty feet up. They were waved in by the guards at the front door, five of them with submachine guns hanging on leather straps around their necks, and passed through a metal detector just inside the doorway to the building. It rang out a beeping alarm.

"Okay, pal, take it out—all your hardware," the leader of the two said, stopping and staring at Stone with dead eyes.

"But I'm not even carrying anything," Stone said. Suddenly he remembered his boots; there was a snub-nosed .38 in one and a blade in the other. He reached down and took them out and handed them over grudgingly. He didn't like being without any weapons, not in the new America. They passed him through again and this time the beeper remained silent. He was led down a hall as white and sterile as the hospital had been and into a small five-sided room surrounded by mirrors on every wall. An armchair sat in the dead center of the room, which made Stone feel slightly dizzy, as if its extra wall somehow set it out of a normal three-dimensional perspective and set his nerves off center.

"Please be seated," one of the I.S. men said, pointing to the chair. Stone glanced down at it to make sure no stakes or snakes were waiting, and seeing nothing plopped down into it, glad of the chance to rest his overloaded stomach for a second.

"Someone will be right in," the man said with a grim,

darting glance and the two of them turned, quickly exiting the room. Stone sat silently in the chair, looking around the room. With the mirrors from floor to ceiling on every wall the illusion created was of endless images of him in the chair receding into infinity, five infinities, for the image was reflected from every angle. The overall effect was as if one were falling into oneself forever. It made him feel dizzy, as if he were flying into his own mind. He knew also that he was being observed; behind one or perhaps all the mirrors men were watching him, perhaps taking pictures. The whole thing was a test. But for what?

Stone suddenly heard a sharp metallic sound and felt bands shoot up around his wrists and ankles. He struggled hard, but he was instantly and completely sealed in by steel wraps that felt unbreakable. The chair whirred deep inside and began stretching out, moving. Within seconds it had spread out until it was flat—and he was on his back unable to move an inch.

"Ah, so sorry to inconvenience you, Mr. Stone," a voice said as a doorway in one of the mirrors opened and a man stepped through. He came toward the prisoner with slow, relaxed steps until he stood right over Stone. He smiled down—the smile a rattler has when he spots a prairie dog a foot from his mouth. Stone suddenly wished he was back in the wastelands where they never smiled. "But we do have to be careful," the I.S. officer said softly. "I'm sure you can understand."

"Oh, of course," Stone answered, looking up, squinting since lights overhead made it difficult to see. "I don't mind at all being strapped down to a moving armchair and immobilized like a pig about to be slaughtered. The only thing I do mind is now you've added armchairs to my list of things to be paranoid about. From now on I'll never be able to sit down in one without shooting it first."

"Ah, very amusing." The man laughed, more of a gurgle than a normal laugh. "It's good to have a sense of humor. Shows the signs of a superior intelligence. Allow me to introduce myself. I'm Colonel Spears, head of the I.S. unit. Yours is a slightly unusual case, and being unusual of course it attracts the attention of our security people. We just want to go over a few things. Usually we do most of our recruiting from the towns—more stable environments. Much of the refuse we've picked up on the road, in the wilds, have proved to be undesirable ultimately. You were actually rescued from a kill zone, and probably would have been eliminated had you been doing anything but dying. But, paradox of paradoxes, we rescued you instead of killing you."

He reached below the chair and extracted a syringe from a hidden drawer.

"Torture time? Bamboo beneath the fingernails?" Stone asked as he saw the big needle rising back up into the air.

"Oh, hardly." Colonel Spears laughed again. Stone didn't like it when he laughed. It made his rodentlike face with slicked-back black hair and angular cheekbones even more ratlike. "We're very efficient here. That's the rule of the game under General Patton—efficiency. There are ways to find out the truth far better and more reliable than bone bending." He squeezed the plunger slightly and a little stream of clear liquid squirted up into the air. He lowered the syringe to Stone's shoulder and plunged the tip in. Stone winced for a fraction of a second. He hated fucking needles. He'd rather get shot than stuck with that long ice pick.

"Sodium pentothal," the colonel said, injecting a shitload of the stuff into Stone's veins. He stood back and looked down paternally at his clamped-down subject. Stone found himself quickly falling under an avalanche of pressure in his brain. It just kept pushing him down until his consciousness felt like it was in his feet.

"Name?" Spears asked.

"Stone, Martin Stone," Stone heard his own lips numbly reply. It was as if he was watching it from beneath the water, a hundred feet down, watching his mouth move high above, and he couldn't do a thing about it.

"Born?" Spears asked, as he glanced down at a digital readout of a sophisticated lie detector that sampled Stone's pulse and body heat and veni-pressure from detectors within the steel clamps.

"Denver, Colorado." Stone's mouth answered while Stone looked up from the bottom of a mental quarry.

"Reason for being in the Green River." Spears asked.

"I fell-fell in," the Stone mouth answered.

"Reason for being here in Fort Bradley," the I.S. chief asked, pacing around slowly in front of Stone. As he asked each question Spears glanced up to watch Stone's facial reactions and also the readouts on the monitor set below the now horizontal chair.

"No . . . rea—reason," Stone's lips dumbly whispered. "Was being treated for bite wound. Just woke up today. No reason. No reason." He kept mumbling like a broken robot, as if his chemically altered, momentarily lobotomized brain couldn't quite understand the concept of "reason." He was just here. That was all. There was no reason for it. It was all very existential or something.

"Are you a cannibal?" Spears asked, looking sharply at Stone's face, which registered extreme repugnance.

"God, no," the voice answered, and Stone cheered it on from his observation point down in his toes. That was true

—score a point for his side. "I've never touched human flesh, or my dog either. Both of us would rather eat ants."

Spears laughed again. "Even under pentothal, a sense of humor. Remarkable, Mr. Stone, you have an extremely strong will and personality to exhibit even that much independence. I gave you a large dose." Colonel Spears went on and on, flashing him quick questions about any number of things.

"Are you a homosexual? Do you have any diseases? How much money do you possess?" And Stone answered truthfully to all—"no," "no," "none."

"How many men have you killed?" Spears asked suddenly, moving up to the lie detecting monitor for close inspection of the waveform results.

"Too many to count," Stone's mouth replied.

"More than ten?"

"Yes."

"More than fifty?"

"Yes."

"More than a hundred?"

"I would imagine so," Stone's mouth answered.

"Tell me, Mr. Stone," the I.S. chief asked, as he stood right over the elongated chair and stared down into Stone's face, checking every muscle, every hint of facial expression. "Just how have you been able to kill so many? You don't on the surface look like a master killer."

"However I look," Stone's voice answered with an almost bored weariness, "I have killed a number of men. Killing comes easily to me. I was trained by one of the masters of killing, my father, Major Clayton Stone." He paused and then went on slowly, enunciating each word almost syllable by syllable—one of the effects of the truth serum. "I was told by the shaman of a tribe of Ute Indians who saved my life several months ago that I was a *nadi*, one with the gift of giving death."

"Final question, Mr. Stone," the colonel said with his razor-edged grin. "Why have you killed so many men?"

"Because they tried to kill me," Stone answered, almost in a whisper now, as the drug was starting to send him under.

Spears bent down and looked closely at the green line that undulated across the monitor screen, studying its every curve closely. At last he stood up fully. "You know, some men can actually learn to fool both pentothal and lie detector. But not many. Not many at all. I think you're telling the truth."

"I am t—t—telling the truth," Stone's mouth stuttered, trying not to slobber as his lips were starting to feel like slime-coated elephant's ears flapping wetly against one another.

"Well, that's all," Spears said. He closed hinged steel doors over the lie detector below and pressed a button on the side. The chair began slowly folding up like an accordion until it was a chair again. The hand clasps slid into the sides. Stone was free. Even down in his drug-dazed cavern of a brain he liked that idea.

CHAPTER
Ten

STONE STUMBLED back to the hospital. The two I.S. men who'd taken him in walked along on each side of him, holding him as he started weaving too much to one side of the street. But he just shook them off. He'd walk back on his own if he had to crawl. At last the words FORT BRADLEY HOSPITAL FOR SURGERY crawled into his eyeballs and Stone pushed through the door. Nurse Williamson was waiting in the lobby and took him from the custody of the Cro-Mags. Stone was glad to see them go.

"Come on," she said, taking her patient by the arm. "You look like hell. Let's get you to bed." Her he let lead him. Even in his stupor the feel of her flesh, her warmth against him, felt wonderful. She opened a door, snapped on a light and half threw him down on the bed, where he landed right on his face and stomach. She quickly undressed him and got him under the covers. His body was nearly as limp as a rag doll now as the entire load of truth serum circulated through his veins, acting much like a dose of barbiturates. She injected him quickly with several shots of God knew what all. Even in his zombie state Stone was getting pissed off at how many drugs were being pumped into his flesh. It was getting a little ridiculous.

But then she pulled the covers over him and turned off the lights. He fell asleep within seconds into a mercifully dark and, for the moment, safe pit of unconsciousness. But already paranoid images filled his dreams. The eagle, the golden eagle of the I.S. unit, dozens of them were flying down out of a storm-filled sky. And in the blood-dripping claws of each one, a human skull, the prunelike faces shriveled back in shrunken head screams of total horror . . . then they dove for his skull.

He woke, kicking and shaking his fists. He was surrounded by feathers and beaks.

"No, no, it's me, relax," a voice said from out of the darkness. Stone opened his puffy eyes and saw Nurse Williamson in the dim glow of a night-light across the room. "You had a bad dream. You were shivering. Here, I'll put another blanket on you. It got very cold suddenly outside— must be an arctic front coming in." She grabbed a navy blue hospital blanket from a nearby closet and unfolded it, spreading it over him with a quick throw. She came around to the front of the bed.

"There, is that better—" she started to ask. Without really being aware of what he was doing—just wanting her— Stone reached out and grabbed her, arms pulling her down on top of him. She landed on his chest, their two bodies touching at every point. She resisted at first. But as she felt the warmth, the need of his body to be next to hers, she gave in. She could feel something melting inside her, a shield she had put up ever since she had joined the NAA. She hadn't let a man get this close to her since she'd been raped. Not that a lot hadn't tried. But she felt something for Stone. Something inexplicable. And rather than try to leave, she turned her head toward him and sought his lips like a bird too long denied food. And when their tongues touched it was as if she exploded into a bomb of passion.

She pulled herself hard against him, crushing her breasts with all her strength against his lean strong chest. She buried her face in his neck and groaned as his hands stroked up and down her back and along her womanly hips. Suddenly her whole body began jerking uncontrollably as if she were on fire, as if steaming lava were pumping into her veins. She cleaved to him and spread her legs quickly apart and wrapped around one of his thighs. Almost involuntarily she reached down and felt for his hardness and gasped when she found it. It seemed impossible that she could take all of him.

She rose suddenly and undid the zipper on her back and slipped out of her nurse's uniform and let it drop to the floor. Stone looked at her with wide eyes that still had trouble focusing. But from what he could make out, she was a veritable goddess—breasts like pomegranates standing out straight and firm, a thin waist and below glistening treasures that made his own erect staff stand a little taller. She ran over to the door of the recovery room, locking it, and then turned off the light of the supply closet. Now the only source of illumination was a kind of night-light—a five-volt bulb that plugged into the wall, casting a gentle sheet of gold over the entire room.

Suddenly she was back in the bed with him and her body felt like Christmas and the Fourth of July and Polish Independence Day all wrapped up into one. He had felt exhausted when he fell asleep and had slept in a near coma for four hours before stirring from his nightmares. And somehow she made him feel awake. To say the least.

"Come here, nurse," Stone laughed in the dark, reaching for her. "What is your name anyway?"

"Elizabeth," a soft, quavering voice said from beside him on the bed.

"Elizabeth," Stone whispered almost to himself. A beautiful name. She came to him ready to give him the perfect art and beauty of her young body. Her breasts seemed to almost swell as his hands grasped them firmly and he squeezed hard. Her face flushed with desire as she boldly dropped her hand down again and grabbed hold of him. Suddenly, as if under the control of a puppeteer, she began twitching again as her frozen sexual energies unlocked and her muscles filled with jolts of electricity. She slid down his entire body, licking him with her wet pointed tongue, from chest to navel. Then lower.

She kissed his staff, making it spring even higher, as if it had a life of its own. Her tongue rushed over the swollen shaft as a moan of animal pleasure sang softly through her parted lips. Stone could smell the intoxicating aphrodisiac of her aroused golden triangle of fur below. She moved up and down on his stiffness, barely able to take it into her small mouth, but wanting to, trying to. Stone reached down and grabbed her around the already wet mound of fur between her legs. He grabbed hard and squeezed and she responded like a cat in heat, dropping her head down, arching her whole back up. He played with the pink petals of her sex and then pushed a finger deep into her. She seemed to spasm up and let out a whoosh of air, as she clenched and unclenched around him.

Suddenly he reached down and put his hands around her waist, lifting her up toward him as if she were light as a pillow. He pulled her to his chest and then reached down and grabbed behind each of her creamy thighs and pulled her up onto him as he guided the long spear of flesh with one hand into her parted wet lips. She groaned, her eyes shutting tight, her head falling to his shoulder in a swoon as the stiff organ plummeted into her core. She whipped her legs up around his waist to make room for him and locked her ankles together behind his back.

He started pumping into her, slowly at first, and as both their passions heated up, harder and faster until he was like a steam piston of slamming sensation inside of her, her triangle of light blonde hair dripping with the juices of her passions. Stone forced himself ever deeper into her, as if mining for something, some vital part of her soul. He tore into her body, forcing her legs apart, pushing into the darkest recesses of her body, taking her to the very summits of sensation that a woman can know on this earth.

Suddenly she seemed to go into a complete frenzy of movement as waves of super sensation streamed up from her stomach and her clitoris, which grinded against him. Her head slammed back and forth, eyes tightly shut, as the lowest of wildcat growls rumbled through her mouth. Stone could feel his manhood grow even stiffer and longer, hard as hammered steel, and he grabbed her round buttocks, pulling her against him until they felt as if they would merge into one pulsing flesh. His eyes suddenly closed as he felt the thick fluid rise up and surge through the swollen organ, pumping into her with powerful, wild stabs. He erupted in a volcanic explosion of white hot lava shooting into her boiling caverns.

Her entire body went completely rigid and her face paler and paler until it seemed all the blood had drained. Suddenly she sucked in a breath and the blood filled her face again and she let out with a long half scream, half howl of pleasure as her body vibrated around him like a blender trying to take down a whale. It seemed to go forever, her entire body contracting from stomach to breasts, through her thighs. She jerked and vibrated as he thrust into her, and came with the most powerful orgasm she had ever experienced. They groaned simultaneously, and for one glorious second they merged into one being, joined together in mindless, wonderful animal bliss.

CHAPTER
Eleven

WHEN HE awoke again she was gone. The place in the bed by his side was still warm but her body was gone. She had run from him in fear. Women were like that sometimes when they felt they had enjoyed themselves too much the night before. The superego reasserted itself over the inner animal passions. But the animal would rise again. The superego would be hurled aside, and she would again come again.

He felt almost one hundred percent. The poison had run its course through his body, making love with Elizabeth had restored him, had recharged his body. That's why a man needs a woman—to replenish his battery with power. There is nothing like it. Nothing. Who could say how or why. But touching her, being inside her, had healed him. The perfumes of a woman's body were more medicinal than all the sterile bottles science had to offer. Even his hand, which he lifted and looked at, was losing its ghastly black-and-purple color and returning to a reddish pink. The swelling had subsided completely. He still had a little trouble bending it, but it worked.

He had scarcely had time to dwell on sweet musings of the night before when there was a loud knocking on the door. A barrel-chested sergeant with clipboard and drill instructor's hat barged into his room. He had a face like a squashed pumpkin—like something that had been stepped on a few too many times—and huge cauliflower ears with what appeared to be worm holes embroidering their edges.

"Training has begun. Report to the parade field in five minutes. And please don't be late," the man screamed with a mock sarcasm of politeness. Stone stared after the sergeant as he pulled the door shut hard and stomped out, waking half the patients in the place. Before he knew it he found himself up and dressing. He hadn't even decided what the hell he was going to do. But his curiosity was aroused. In a way he wondered just what the training was like. Besides, there was a lot about this whole operation that confused him no end. There was nothing he could put his finger on but something was wrong somewhere. Or was it just his fucking cynical core that found it so hard to believe that all these guys were for real, that he had found the kind of people he had been searching for. Stone couldn't even tell anymore; his intuitive distant early warning system seemed to have blown a fuse.

He headed out of the building and walked down the main asphalt road that led through the center of Fort Bradley. Stone made his way over to the twenty-five recruits who stood in slightly uneven lines facing a pole that held the flag of the NAA, crossed M-16's over the stars and stripes, this one a good six by seven feet in dimensions and hand-stitched with vivid red and blue and white—and a silver metallic sheen for the rifles. It whipped loosely around in the breeze, about thirty feet above their heads. Stone got into one of the back rows. A few hours of calisthenics would be good, he thought to himself. Stretch him out. Get things shook up in there a little.

The drill sergeant waited impatiently, looking at his watch and then his clipboard. At last two more men came running down the street pulling on their jackets and settled into place.

"Now, gentlemen, you are about to make the magical transformation from idiot into fighting soldier. We don't go about training the usual way here. Instead we have what we call the make-it-or-break-it method. This is, gentlemen, for the next two days you are going to be pushed until every cell in your body is ready to explode; you will run and fight and climb and build until you think your feet are going to turn to porridge and your legs to rubber bands. But still you're going to go on, because I'll be right behind you, ready to kick you in the ass should you slow down. But mostly you're going to to go because you WANT to be a member of the most illustrious fighting force in America today. Don't you, idiots?"

"Yes sir," a few of the recruits in the first row spoke out.

"WHAT'S THAT?" the D.I. screamed so loudly back at them that a dog nearly half a mile away in the pens started barking.

"YES SIR," every one of them shouted back, standing bolt upright, backs ramrod stiff. Even Stone joined in. Sort of.

The D.I. walked back and forth in front of them, a huge Polack, with a face like a cow and a body and shoulders that looked like they could lift one. "I'm Sergeant Zynishinski. Don't try to pronounce my name, just say 'sergeant' whenever you want to address me. I'm the guy who runs this forty-eight-hour marathon training. General Patton has his own ideas of war. If you get through this, you're for us. If not, it's better to find out now. You're going to hate my guts by the time we're through. And wish you could send a how-itzer on my head or run a bayonet through me. And you know what, I'll give you the opportunity to try it. But first" —he looked into their apprehensive faces and snorted out a sigh of disgust. Then he spat a cupcake-sized gob of spittle onto the dirt. "Let's start with the basics."

"First the sacred oath of our army. This oath is signed and sealed in blood. Only blood binds us together so that we can't be broken." He handed a knife to the men at each end of the three lines. "These are the direct words of General Patton himself, gentlemen idiots: 'It is our common sacrifice of blood on the field of battle that makes us one, unites us in the war on evil,'" He looked around at them, making sure they knew how to use the damned blades.

"Now, cut yourself and when you all have blood coming out, put your bleeding fist over your heart." He sliced his arm, which Stone saw had been cut over and over again so the forearm had healed into a scarred purple surface as jagged and ugly as the stark face of the moon. Each man sliced himself and passed the knife down the line. Some of them did it with eyes open, others with eyes shut tight as doors; some sliced their own flesh as if carving a piece of bologna, others stabbed forward into palm or wrist or arm, wanting to get it over with fast. A few just cut into them-selves with total detachment, sawing as if they were slicing up a roast and had forgotten if it was a quarter or half pound they were cutting up. Groans and gasps chorused through the men but not a one screamed, not in front of their fellow initiates.

Stone took the knife when it was handed to him and stared

at it. He looked over the sergeant, who had already placed his bleeding forearm over his chest so that drops fell onto his uniform and down onto the ground. What the hell, Stone thought, trying to muster his own shield of grim detachment. When in Rome, as they used to say. He placed it against the front of his forearm on the outside fleshy part and nicked the tip in about a half inch and then sliced forward for about two inches.

"Shiiiit," he hissed, gritting his teeth together, snapping his eyes suddenly shut in pain. He looked down. There was a reasonable amount, Stone decided, as a stream of red flowed slowly out as if through a crack in a dam. He handed the blade onto the next man. Within a minute and a half they had all made their cuts.

"Now face the flag of the NAA," the D.I. said, turning toward the fluttering symbol of military strength that snapped in a sudden gust of wind. "Now swear after me, swear on your own blood allegiance to our flag. And repeat after me. I—say your name."

"I, Martin Stone," Martin said, trying to get into the spirit of the thing. But not quite able.

"Swear total and complete obedience to the New American Army, its commander General Patton and all its officers." They repeated his words, some stumbling over them. Some of the more uneducated ones from the sticks were a little slow at this sort of thing and kept looking at the D.I. in horror, afraid that they would make a dumb mistake.

"And I pledge to give my life for my fellow soldier, just as I give my blood today."

"—give my blood today," they echoed after him.

"And I swear to carry out all the orders I am given, whatever they entail."

"—whatever they entail," they barked back.

"Now, walk to the base of the flag, one at a time, and throw some of your blood on the rocks. You'll see where; it's red with the blood of all the men who've come through these gates. You're joining not just the men of this army, but also our ghosts. The spirits of our fighting past. This is the most sacred oath you're ever going to make, so leave now if you can't hold up your end. There's no backing out later."

They walked forward one by one and waved their arms around at the base of the flagpole until a few drops or sprinkles fell atop the faded waxy buildup of red—the blood from a thousand veins. It came Stone's turn and he stopped and hesitated just before the rocks. There was something in him that didn't want to do it, didn't want to swear in blood to anything. Yet it was too late to pull out now. The ghosts of his ancestors would just have to kick the ass of the ghosts of the Third Army if it came to it. He shook his arm and a whole thimblefull of blood sluiced down and made a plopping sound on the rocks. Stone looked around proudly at his contribution but the others were all too engrossed in their own mental trips, their eyes locked on another dimension—the past, the history of their own lives—for they were about to enter a new life, to change forever. And who could say how they would turn out or what their fates would be.

"You are now official recruits of the New American Army. And God be with you." Sergeant Zynishinski said the final words in a kind of undertone that made them sound quite ominous. And the recruits started wondering just what they'd gotten themselves into.

"That was the easy part; now comes the fun," the D.I. said, turning to look at them with the happy eyes of a panther when it spots a gazelle sunning itself on a nearby rock. "First, let's do a little running—just to get ourselves loosened up. Now count off. One after another."

The recruits, after staring at one another in confusion but at last getting it going, counted off from one to twenty-five. Stone was twenty-three. Way in the back, just the way he liked it.

"Now one line is evens, the other odds. You got that, you idiots?"

"Yes sir," the recruits screamed back.

"Now odds step out and come up alongside the trooper in front of you." They looked confused and stumbled around in front of one another for a few seconds. "Jesus God, have you sent me the dumbest of the dumb—cows instead of men," Sergeant Zynishinski asked his own private god as he glared up with a look of wary disgust at the dawn sky just starting to paint itself in with pastel oranges and faded reds. When they were at last paired off, he started jogging around the parade ground, a rectangle about two football fields long that had been cleared down to a thin layer of dead brown grass, which just gave it the tiniest bit of a cushion against their boots.

The D.I. kept it going, setting into a medium, even pace and took them around the track. The recruits smiled confidently at one another. If this was it, it was going to be a snap.

"This it—this as fast as your running exercise here get?" a mountain boy with a long drawl asked as he ran in the front row just behind the mountain-sized instructor who slammed on like an elephant a yard ahead.

"This is it, boy," the D.I. grunted back. They ran around the circumference of the long field back to where they had started and then continued on another round. By the end of the second completion—each complete go-around equaling about half a mile—some of the men were already starting to huff and puff a little. But they sucked in and just pushed harder.

And they ran. And ran. And ran. After half an hour, some of them started to grow impatient, restless. But the sergeant wasn't answering questions, just running ahead of them, pulling them relentlessly on. After an hour, half of them were dragging their feet on the ground. Even at the slow jogging pace they couldn't go on. Yet they had to. By the end of the second hour, every man's face was beet red, his lungs heaving. By the end of the third hour, they would have welcomed a heart transplant.

At last the sergeant stopped and turned to them. He wasn't even breathing all that hard. "Five minute rest. So meditate or masturbate—or say your prayers. 'Cause that was the easy part."

The men collapsed onto the ground, Stone along with them. Four men lay fallen in heaps of exhaustion around the field. The D.I. walked around to them and sent them off to the debriefing building. They were out. After what seemed like just seconds he came back to them.

"On your feet, assholes. Attention!" They jumped to—or tried to, standing in somewhat shaky lines, praying there would be no more running.

"Now we learn how to kill. Which one of you idiots thinks you can kick my ass?" He glanced around challengingly, trying to catch a pair of responsive eyes. "Come on now, you're all tough bastards, right? I mean that's why you've volunteered, 'cause you want to kick ass." The recruits looked around at one another, wondering who would be fool enough to try. In their own villages and ramshackle towns, each had been one of the toughest in the teeth-smashing brawls on Saturday night when they got loaded up with rotgut at what passed for the local tavern. Here they were just another cow in the herd and their toughness suddenly seemed to have become somewhat laughable.

At last one huge fellow, nearly as large as the sergeant, stepped forward. "I might just give that offer a try," he said with a swagger that suggested he had seen his share of fights—and had won them all."

"Well, mightn't you, now?" Sergeant Zynishinski replied with a happy little smile on his thick-lipped mouth. "Well, please be my guest." He waved his hand at the ground in front of him as if bowing and stepped back a few feet. "What's your name, my brave idiot," the sergeant asked. "So's I can know who I'm about to knock down?"

"Name's Gatlin. But back where I come from they all just call me 'Bull.' Cain't even remember my first name. Ain't nobody called me it for a long, long time. Now I ain't gonna get in no trouble, is I?" the six-four brute asked with narrowed eyes. "That is, when I sets you on your ass?" He glanced around at the recruits with a smirk on his face. They looked at him as if he were insane.

"When you—?" The sergeant laughed with true amusement at the question. "My dear boy, if you can knock me down I guarantee you'll have the thanks and appreciation of most of the men in this fort. No, I promise you," he said, letting his ham-sized hands hang loosely at his sides, "whatever goes on between us, nobody else ever knows about it. My word."

"Well, I guess yo' word is good enough for me." The two of them squared off and the recruits watched with something approaching awe. As each of the challengers weighed in at two-fifty to three hundred pounds it was akin to watching some kind of sumo match. Both had a lot of bulk, but it was the kind that was more muscle than fat. They looked as if they could be hit by a truck and the metal would come out the loser. They circled around once, the challenger throwing out a few quick punches just to see what the reaction would be. But Sergeant Zynishinski didn't even bother to block them, just stepped back an inch or two and the fists stopped inches short of his flesh. Just from the catlike way he moved Stone could tell the man was a fighter of extraordinary dimensions. Nothing extra, just enough movement to get the job done. It was the style of fighting his father had taught him for five years when they were holed up together in the mountain bunker. Only this guy was a master.

Suddenly the recruit made his move, charging in with a series of lefts and rights that would have flattened a rogue rhino. The D.I. blocked them with amazingly fast windshield-wiper-type motions of his arms and then stepped inside the flailing recruit. He brought his right knee up suddenly between the other man's legs—and it was all over. If the recruits had been hoping for a heavyweight boxing match they were disappointed. "Bull" fell to the dirt with his eyes bulging and lay there sucking in hard for air. Elapsed time of battle: 3.6 seconds. After about a half minute the sergeant reached down and helped him up. The still gasping recruit rose, rubbing his affected parts, his eyes still not quite focusing right.

"If I'd wanted to, I could have stopped your family line right then and there," the D.I. said with an almost fatherly expression. "I pulled the blow at the last second. No hard feelings, huh?" He held out his hand and the recruit shook it limply, more out of fear than anything else. It was the first fight he had ever lost.

CHAPTER
Twelve

THE SUN rose high into the afternoon sky, the first really bright day they had had for a week. Fort Bradley was alive with squads of men rushing around; trucks and jeeps tearing this way and that, carrying munitions, food, construction supplies . . . At the northern end of the camp heavy construction was under way to enlarge the borders of the enclosure—more warehouses, more training fields, more electrified barbed-wire fences. In the center of the main parade field, the recruits were learning about the weaknesses of the flesh, the body points to attack, every way that a man could be immobilized—and destroyed.

"These are all combat techniques." The sergeant addressed them as each man squared off with a partner. "This ain't no fisticuffs or karate or any of that bullshit. All we learn here is how to fuck up a man fast. 'Cause there ain't no rules out there—except to survive. And the way YOU survive is to kill the other guy." He showed them all the major points of the body to attack—using fists, feet, knees, elbows—and using Bull as his somewhat reticent practice dummy. Then each man faced his adversary and tried to imitate the move. The sergeant went up and down the rows, bending a knee here, showing how to move in fast by taking a big step, teaching them all the little tips that made the difference between taking someone out and just making them madder and meaner.

Stone was paired off with a recruit nearly as large as Bull, with a squashed-in nose that looked like it had been hit with a sledgehammer. The man was tremendously strong, his muscles bulging through his brown jacket, but he didn't seem like a bad sort and whispered to Stone as they started, "Name's Bo. Let's not try to kill each other, okay pal?"

"Name's Stone," Stone replied. "Sounds like a good idea to me." They each tried out all the moves on one another, careful to not actually use much force—strangleholds, sweeps, throws, and light strikes to the vital pressure points. Stone knew most of the concepts—having been trained by the man who invented some of them—but even he paid close attention, picking up moves here and there that he had never seen before.

The hand-to-hand went on through the middle of the day until at last Sergeant Zynishinski looked at his wristwatch and called a break. "You get a ten-minute break. No food, as much water as you want." He pointed to three buckets of sloshing water that some troopers carried onto the field. "Don't bust a gut." The men hit the precious water like desert animals after a drought. They slurped it up fast so that most of them quickly got stomach cramps and lay back down on the ground moaning.

"All right, enough napping," the D.I. said after exactly ten minutes to the second. "Now, you've learned a little bit about how to fight bare-handed. Forget all of it! Because every son-of-a-bitch out there has a weapon, and so will you." He pulled a huge double-edged commando knife from its sheath by his side and hefted it in his hand. "This is my baby," the D.I. said with something like affection. "It's seen the insides of a lot of men's guts—and sent them all into hell. Bull, you want to come here for a minute." The huge recruit slowly rose with a look of terror on his face.

"You ain't gonna cut me up, is you, Sarge?" he asked with a pleading little-boy tone that was almost comical on such a mashed-in face. But no one laughed.

"Now would I do that?" the sergeant asked with a harsh laugh. "The officers would have me eating pigshit out of a trough if I was to be slicing up all these nice young bodies here." He demonstrated on his somewhat less than enthusiastic "volunteer" the many ways that a blade can do a man in. How to cut an artery, how to strike a disabling blow with a single thrust, coming up from behind and grabbing the head and slicing the throat all in a split second. The recruits saw every bloody way that steel can carve flesh, and then got to try it all out on one another. Two more were lost here—with stab wounds, one to the shoulder, the other right into the cheek. Both would live, but the blood pouring from their wounds meant they were out, *finito*, washed up in the NAA before they had ever begun. Patton wanted only the cream for his forces. And those who survived getting wounded in training were more likely to do the same in combat, as far as he could see. At any rate, he ran the show and thus all of his training concepts were implemented.

Then it was staffs, which the sergeant was clearly as expert with as every other goddamned weapon. He poked and swung away at Bull, showing countless lightning-quick moves that could send a man to the ground like a falling tree. Again, the recruits got to try it all out on one another: a few bloody noses, cracked elbows and wrists along the way. After an hour or two of the practice, the sergeant called a halt to the action and searched around for some subjects.

"Now, let's see what the hell you've learned—if anything. Let's see, how about you, Bull." The man rose and stood next to him, fearing another onslaught of one kind or another. "And"—he glanced around and saw Stone's unflinching eyes staring right back at him while everyone else was looking down at the ground, pretending not to exist. He had noticed that Stone seemed quite adept at all the weapons, unusually good for a raw recruit. "And you!" He handed them each a long oak staff and stood back. "Okay boys, go to it."

Bull looked happy for the first time that afternoon. At last someone whose ass HE could kick. He circled around Stone, holding the stick above his head like a baseball bat looking for a nice round object to smash.

"I ain't gonna hurt you . . . much," the big man snickered and Stone could see dark cruelty in the eyes, a desire to fuck him up bad, a chance to earn back some of the macho that had been stripped off him like a veneer of cracked paint by Sergeant Zynishinski.

"And I promise the same, pal," Stone said quietly back to him. He waited, holding the staff at loose readiness in front of him. Suddenly Bull charged, swinging his staff like a club, as if he were out to split a log in two at the first stroke. But Stone was faster. And when it comes to combat, speed always wins. He parried the strike with what looked like a quick flick of the wrists and then lowered the stick between the huge man's knees. Lumbering forward, Bull didn't have time to stop and, becoming entangled in the staff, fell to the ground with a loud thud. Stone stood back and stared down.

"Told you I wouldn't hurt you." This enraged the bear-sized man to such a degree that his face turned a blazing red and he leapt up again, charging with frantic strokes. This time Stone stepped to the side at the last second as the stick whizzed by his head. He slammed the end of his pole into the big man's stomach, and as Bull whooshed air, came down with the side of it on the back of the man's neck. He struck with minimal force—he didn't want to kill him—and Bull hit the dirt face first, out cold before his nose dug into the ground.

"Jesus, that's pretty fucking good," the D.I. said, stepping over the prone body. "Where the hell did you learn all that stuff?"

"My dad was a Ranger," Stone said with a thin smile. "He taught me a few pointers." Bull came to, shook his head and then realized what had happened to him. He rose again, his face even redder than before if that was possible and started at his adversary again, unable to accept that a shrimp like that could take him down.

"Easy, easy, big fellow," the sergeant said with a laugh. "This guy could've killed you if he wanted. You'll get your chance to let blood out there"—he swept his hand past the fence surrounding the fortress. "Enough of this for now. It's up to each of you: what you learn, what you remember. I won't be out there when you face the bikers and the cannibals and all the other slime that live out in the wastelands. If you do it wrong, you'll find out." He pushed Bull and Stone back into the ranks. Stone saw the man he had just knocked down give him just about the coldest look he had ever seen and heard a whisper through the bloody lips his front teeth had cut when he went down. "I'll kill you, motherfucker—bet on it."

"Now, from hands and knives to the real thing—the

things you'll be using ninety-nine percent of the time you're out there fighting: firearms," the D.I. told them. He had another of the recruits who had been pretty badly banged up sent off under escort of guards, and then led them across the parade grounds to another large field with firing ranges, trenches and a shitload of weaponry—rifles, automatic weapons and even a few cannons.

"Later you'll be given—those of you who make it through—specialized training in your assigned weapons. But for now we want all of you to have at least a working knowledge of all our basic firepower. You never know when you'll be out there and your weapon will jam, and some cocksucker will be coming at you with blood in his eyes. You'd better be able to fire anything that has a trigger. You understand?"

"Yes sir," the recruits shouted back, bleary eyes weary of the hours they'd already put in. But there wasn't the slightest chance for rest as the sergeant started demonstrating the firing, loading, stripping and cleaning of a wide assortment of firearms used by the NAA—M-16A's, Colt AR-15's, Mossberg 12 gauge pumps, Colt .45 combat pistols as well as the NATO 9mm Beretta. They followed suit, taking apart and putting together an assortment of pistols and rifles on tarps on the ground, all under the watchful eye of the D.I. The sergeant strode around, constantly pointing out the correct way, cursing the dumb "lobotomized cows that God had sent him" to start getting it together. After about three hours they were led to the firing range and lay down side by side in a long row. It was already starting to get dark again and there were no lights on the field, just what filtered from the lights of the fortress itself about a quarter mile off. A truck rolled up and a squad of troops jumped out, carrying what looked like bodies.

"We strive for realism here," Sergeant Zynishinski said. "So we ain't got no lives ones, but we do got some dead ones for you to try out on. There ain't nothing like shooting at real flesh—even if it's a little on the rancid side—to give you a feel for what bullets will do to a man. And if it's the first time you're shooting at human flesh, you can do your puking now and get it over with." The recruits blanched, and even Stone felt a little queasy as the corpses were carried out and tied up to poles about a hundred feet from them until there were a dozen of the dead bodies in various states of decomposition tied up and staring back at them through flat dead eyes. Stone wondered but didn't ask where the leftovers had come from, though the pockmarked, ugly faces of the recently deceased didn't look like they had been people you would want to invite home to dinner even when they had been alive.

They each got themselves in a comfortable position approximating the way the sergeant had demonstrated and sighted up their M-16's. The rifle was the more advanced 9mm model, but Stone didn't really like the feel of it. It had always had a bad rep, but this was what the Third Army had to use, so he used it. He sighted up the corpse directly ahead of him, getting a bead right between the eyes. Then he corrected for what he sensed was a slightly downward push of the sights. The other men all squinted madly down their barrels.

"Remember what I told you about vital points," the sergeant said, stepping back behind the recruits who lay prone on the dirt, elbows on the ground. "Shoot the motherfuckers!" he yelled. And the firing squad of recruits opened up with everything they had. Stone pulled the trigger and the rifle jerked with a satisfying recoil. The head of Stone's corpse seemed to suddenly have a rather large hole missing in the center of its chalky face—where the eyes and nose had once lived. Then other parts of it took hits as the men fired again and again. Fingers blasted off, teeth and ears flew into the air, spiraling from the hit of the 9mm slugs. Arms and legs seemed to jump and whip around in the air, as if they were dancing to some tune inaudible to human ears, as bullets tore into them. Slowly they were ripped apart as whole sections of them disappeared from their bodies. After five minutes there was hardly anything left except a pink gruel that coated the stakes, and various unrecognizable red things lying around the ground.

"Excellent, excellent," the D.I. said, as he halted the rifle practice and moved them along to the grenade range about one hundred feet to the right of the corpse targets. He showed the proper holding, arming and throwing of the grenade, of which the fort had a surplus. Each man was given one and then lined up behind a sandbagged protective wall that shielded the whole team. Then, one at a time, they threw them. The grenades were live, and every throw was followed by a sharp snapping explosion and a little spray of dust that trickled back to them through the now dark sky. Stone armed and threw his and ducked down. He had used them before. He liked grenades. Anything that could take out five guys at a time was all right in his book.

One idiot—one of the very last—apparently didn't quite get the message. He pulled the pin and then turned to the sergeant. "Now what the hell . . . I supposed to do next?" The straw-chewer asked with a puzzled look. Even the D.I.'s face drained of blood and he stuttered to throw the fucking thing away. The kid got the message at the last second and heaved the pineapple out over the wall. It went off six feet from his chest. Somehow he lived. But the grenade had sent out a veritable wall of minute shrapnel—and it had almost skinned the thrower alive. The whole right side of his face, shoulder and chest had been razored down to a bloody layer of muscle tissue. "Gosh sorry, Sarge," the kid kept mumbling over and over as he lay on the ground. He kept mumbling it even as medics carried him off on a stretcher, a trail of blood dripping all the way across the field like a highway stripe to hell.

"That's what happens to assholes," Sergeant Zynishinski said, addressing the recruits. "Always know where your weapon is, where your asshole is, and don't confuse the two." He stopped and counted how many were left after the various accidents of training. Eighteen out of an original twenty-five. "My, we're losing men tonight. Well, let's see how many more we can lose. It's beddy bye. Let's go."

"Thank God, we get to sleep," Bo, the man he had been working out with earlier, said to Stone as they jogged side by side across the field.

"Somehow I think sleep is going to be a very tiring experience," Stone answered dryly. The D.I. led them to a stretch of muddy ground along the inside of the fence. The recent rains had make it thick like taffy so that the men could walk on it but if they stopped for very long they started slowly shifting around as their feet corkscrewed down into the giving surface. A truck was waiting for them at the far end of the swampy field, and two NAA supply men handed out a shovel and a tarp to each man.

"Now dig," the sergeant ordered, staring at them with his arms folded. " 'Cause this is the only chance you're going to have to rest for—let's see,"—he looked at his watch—"five hours. Dig foxholes for yourselves. I don't think I have to demonstrate how. If you're too stupid to do what a mole does without thinking, then you deserve whatever happens to you. And if you can, sleep. I'll be back in five. I have to go have me some whiskey—and a steak, I'm hungry as a bear." The sergeant laughed at them, just to rub it in a little more. "Oh, by the way," he shouted as he walked off, "there will be two machine-gun posts watching you at all times, and every once in a while they're going to let loose with a stream of slugs about two inches above the ground. So dig deep. Dig deep." He chuckled again as he headed off, leaving them to their own devices.

"I ain't going to dig no damned foxhole," several voices whispered to one another through the semi-darkness. The men were tired, starving, feeling rebellious and ready to kill. Stone didn't pay them any heed. He tied the tarp around his waist, found the least muddy spot he could and slammed the shovel in. Although the ground was muddy it was a thick hard mud, almost half-frozen with the rapidly dropping temperature as the moon popped up half-hidden behind a tree and a north wind blew down from the great Arctic steppes. It was hard going, like shoveling almost dried cement, but he was able to get some small amount of the stuff with each load.

"Say mister," Bo said, wandering over to him with a sheepish expression on his face, somehow sensing that while the others boldly proclaimed that they were tired of working and weren't going to move a muscle, Stone was one of the few who really knew what he was doing. "You think maybe me and you could team up for the night; you know, make a foxhole together?" It was obvious that the kid didn't know shit about shinola. But though huge, he seemed basically like a decent guy. Stone took pity on him—with a frame that big he'd surely take a hit when the machine guns started firing.

"Sure, Bo, just start digging," Stone said as he took another shovelful. "The quicker we get our condo built the quicker we can get some shut-eye." Bo wasn't quite sure what a condo was but smiled at the acceptance of his company and slammed into the thick mud and dirt with a vengeance. Some of the others kept up their I-ain't-gonna-do-shit attitude, but many of the recruits took Stone's cue, teamed up and started digging. Within ten minutes Stone and his roommate had created a space about eight by six by two, just big enough for the two of them to squeeze in and—if they kept their asses down—wake up with their flesh intact.

The sides of the hole kept slowly sliding down but Stone took his tarp, spread it over as much of the inside of the space as he could. It seemed to help. They both got inside and after getting all their feet and legs in the right place it appeared usable. The mud squished beneath Stone's tarp, making them feel like they were lying on a waterbed, but it kept out the water oozing in the dirt just below them. All the recruits who were digging kept glancing over at Stone to make sure they were doing it right, and followed suit, putting down their tarps over as much of the muddy interior as possible.

"Now give me your tarp," Stone told Bo, who handed it over. Sitting up, Stone placed it on each side of the ditch over them and put some of the mud along the edges to hold it in place. Then he pulled his head back under, pulling the tarp along with him over his head until they were almost sealed in. Within minutes their body heat began collecting so that they actually felt warm.

The rest mimicked Stone down to the last detail. Then they all got in, pulled the movable roof tarp over them and presto: instant home with all the amenities. Bull and three of the "tough guys" of the lot who had sat on their tarps watching it all and making obscene comments at the assholes who were doing more work suddenly heard loud clicking sounds coming from the shadows at each end of the mud field. Suddenly a hailstorm of slugs came migrating across the ground. The four macho men dove into the dirt, pressing their faces into the earth for dear life as they could hear countless bullets whistling by overhead. The firing kept up for nearly two minutes. At last it stopped and a voice yelled out from the darkness.

"That time we fired a yard above the ground. Next time it's going to be twelve inches. Get your foxholes built, assholes." But Bull and the others had gotten the message. They teamed up and grabbed their shovels and started digging like steam shovels. Within ten minutes they had likewise created underground homes that, following Stone's design, were not all that uncomfortable, considering. The next machine-gun burst came exactly fifteen minutes after the first. And true to word, it was a foot off the ground. Someone whose ass was poking up just a little too high took a flesh wound and let out a quick scream. They all pulled down a little deeper, squashed their faces a little harder into the mud-bulging tarps and lay motionless in the oozing holes as a thin drizzle descended through the now moonless night like a dark gossamer veil of the gods. And thus, some of them were even able to get a little sleep between machine-gun firings.

CHAPTER
Thirteen

WAKEUP CALL was two small artillery shells going off at each side of the mud field, ripping the recruits from their semi-dozes and making over half of them bolt upright, so they sat up straight and ripped the tarps from right over their heads.

"That's the WRONG thing to do, idiots," Sergeant Zynishinski screamed at them as he stood in the center of the vaguely circular pattern of foxholes. "When you hear an explosion, get your head DOWN, not up. Now everybody rise and shine 'cause today's the day we *really* have some fun." The men groaned and burped and farted and slowly emerged from their muddy holes in the earth like zombies rising from the dead. And with their mud-splattered clothes, their hair covered with dead grass and twigs—a few of them even sporting various species of beetles and grubs that had crawled onto them during the night, seeking warmth and perhaps a few bites of something tasty—they looked like something out of a horror movie, like something that should just crawl back into its grave and die.

The sergeant walked back and forth in front of them, inspecting the recruits. "So you cowbrains figured out to stay dry. Better than I expected," he commented, spitting a gob of the chewing tobacco he seemed to always have in his mouth at their feet. "And maybe you even got a few minutes sleep, that's good. Because you'll need everything you got for today—everything."

"What about food," one whining voice asked from somewhere.

"No food," the sergeant said brusquely. "All right, let's go. Leave the tarps and shovels where they are. Follow me!" The D.I. started jogging off and Stone and Bo took off right behind him, followed grudgingly by the rest of the trainees. They ran along the side of the electric fence, about two yards from it. Along the bottom Stone could see blankets of dead insects—moths, flies, wasps—that had touched the high-voltage wire. Here and there along the outside was a dead animal—raccoon, prairie dog, even a deer or two. Their faces were still stuck to the steel-mesh structure as the current created a magnetic pull between their bodies and the electricity surging through the metal. Stuck forever as if kissing that which had killed them.

Sergeant Zynishinski led them right up to the side gate, protected by two guard posts on each side. The guards shut off the electricity for their section, opened the gate, let them all through and when the last man was out closed it again and started the current up. There had been a number of attacks lately. They couldn't afford to slacken for a moment. It was the first time Stone had been outside the walls of Fort Bradley in almost a week—and it felt wonderful. He hadn't realized how cramped being inside of walls made him until he was out. But the bush land and nearby forest gave him a sudden jolt of joy. They ran for about half a mile down a dirt road and then came to a clearing with a number of NAA troops gathered around, along with various vehicles, including a tank parked on the grassy shoulder to the side.

"This is it," the D.I. said. "You went to school yesterday; today is the graduation exam." He pointed toward what looked like hardly more than a deer trail leading off through some low thorn bushes. "That's the test. We call it the "manbreaker," because it's broken plenty, believe me. It's an obstacle course. But like none you've ever seen or heard about. This one's different. But I'm not going to tell you all about it and spoil the fun. That's for you to find out. Suffice it to say, you will be forced to use everything you learned yesterday—and every other bit of knowledge you got crammed into those amoeba-sized brains." He looked around at them as if he had never seen a more incompetent gathering of fools and shook his head with mock sadness.

"There are arrows pointing the way. Just follow them. If you get wounded or maimed, stay where you are. We'll get to you when we can—if we can. See you on the other side, idiots. If you make it all the way, you're in this man's army." The big trooper's face softened for just a second. "Good luck," he mumbled. Then with gusto, "Now get your dumb asses in there . . . and keep your fucking heads down." Stone walked up to the first arrow pointing into the thorn patch, breathed out to relax himself and started in. Behind him Sergeant Zynishinski was already in a jeep and heading off down one of the several roads that intersected at the clearing. The rest of the recruits followed one by one after Stone, looking paranoically around although there was nothing more than a few birds diving for insects amongst the vegetation, chirping angrily at the humans who dared disturb them.

It was easy going at first but after several minutes Stone found that the thorns got thicker and longer, their entangled branches higher and harder to push through. The tips of the barbs kept biting into his legs, nipping little stabs into his flesh. Seeing that it only got thicker ahead, Stone stopped in his tracks, took off the heavy NAA combat jacket and spread it around as much of his lower part of his body as he could, tying the sleeves of the garment around his ankles. It was a strange arrangement and made it hard for him to move, almost like being in a potato sack. But it worked, for as he moved on ahead, the jacket protected him from ninety percent of the thorns and the extra protection enabled him to force his way right through the ripping plants as if he were armor-plated. The others behind him took heed and followed suit and the whole crew stomped on behind their involuntary leader.

The thorns lasted for about a half mile, then were gone. Stone saw a sign with an arrow and moved on ahead onto a one-lane dirt road that passed between two low mountains. He started jogging at a slow speed, letting everything hang loose. He was still sore as hell from the events of yesterday and he didn't want to cramp up. The other recruits stumbled out of the thorns and took off after him. They had all come to depend on Stone for knowing what the hell to do, and didn't want to be left behind. Bo came up beside him, running hard, and Stone grinned over at the man who stood inches over him but couldn't have been over seventeen. Bo grinned back. He should've been out feeding the cows, Stone thought with pity, rather than out here learning how to kill men. The guy didn't have it cut out for him.

"Why you here, Bo?" Stone huffed as he heard other recruits breathing hard yards behind them. "What the hell the NAA have that you want?"

"Well, Mr. Stone." The mountain lad thought hard for a second, keeping an even pace alongside of him. "Tell you the truth, I probably wound't be here exceptin' a gang of bikers came through my hills, killed my ma, pa, all my brothers—I had nine of 'em. No sisters. I come back from hauling coon, and there was no one left. Just bloody carcasses with—with their scalps missing." Stone's head jerked when he heard the words.

"Scalps were missing? Well, I can tell you one thing if it's any consolation at all: the man who did that to them is dead; I killed him with my own hands. His name was Straight, named after the straight razors of which he carried dozens."

Bo could hardly believe the words but was too dimwitted to even imagine Stone might be lying. "I—I—I'm grateful for that," Bo stuttered, almost faltering for a second and losing pace. "I ain't one for words, but if I wasn't a man I'd cry from them words you just tol' me. I thank you. I won't forget it."

But there wasn't time for emotional displays, for as the last man came out of the bramble thickets, the first explosion hit just behind them. Then another. Stone picked up speed and the rest followed behind. They tore down the road as there was no place really to hide on the steep rocky slopes of the mountains on each side. Still the explosions followed them—going off just behind them or to one side—and Stone realized they were being channeled, guided like hamsters, made to run with exploding prods. The thought disgusted him, but he sure as hell didn't slow down. They followed the road for a half hour and the barrage didn't let up; if anything it came closer so they had to haul ass as if they were doing wind sprints. After another five minutes of full-blast running, just as they came to the end of the five-mile-long valley, the shelling stopped. The air seemed bizarrely quiet with the explosions gone and each man could hear his own heart beating like a metronome gone mad.

Stone rested for exactly one minute, knowing there would be something to prod them along soon enough. He saw the next arrow sign pointing toward a fairly thick forest about a hundred yards off and headed toward it. None too soon. For those who had dawdled two stench bombs landed in their midst, sending out an acrid, nauseating odor that made them gag and vomit as they staggered toward the woods. But the moment he reached the edge of the dark forest—a canopy of twisted leafless branches woven into a maze of wooden webbing—Stone saw that this wasn't going to be so easy either. Stakes filled the forest floor with what looked like excrement or something foul smeared on their pointed tips. They were everywhere. It appeared that the godlike beings who were guiding their every move wanted them to play Tarzan for a while.

Stone started up the side of the nearest good-sized tree and then along a branch that extended nearly thirty feet into the forest and mingled with the other high branches. He started along it and though the branch shook up and down slightly it was thick enough to hold him. The branch of another tree was just within reach and he grasped it and jumped across to the other. It wobbled wildly but as Stone hung upside like a bat for a few seconds, the branch slowed down and he oozed out a sigh of relief. The wooden stakes below stared up at him with sharp eyes that seemed to see right into his heart. At least the concept worked. He edged down the branch to the middle trunk of the tree, still about twenty feet up, and searched around through the smaller branches for another bark bridge on which to continue his journey forward.

Most of the other recruits, after doing a double take when they saw Stone do his monkey man thing into the trees, started up after him, following the exact route he was taking. A few, of course, Bull included, had to try things the hard way first. They started into the forest, walking on the ground, trying to weave their way between the spears that appeared to grow out of the hard soil. But it was no go. They had scarcely gone ten feet when Bull, in the lead, got wedged in between two chest-high sets of spikes. When he pulled back one of them ripped into his upper arm, going in a good two inches. He howled and ripped it out and then slowly pulled out backwards. Though he hated Stone and everything he did, Bull knocked the next guy on line out of the way and started up the first tree.

With Stone in the lead, whether he wanted it or not, the entire crew made their way through the high branches of the forest. It was rough going. Especially for the larger men, whose weight seemed to pull the branches to their limits. But somehow it all held, and slowly, like aged gorillas who had forgotten quite how to do it, they headed along branch by branch, tree by tree, through the spider web of wood. It seemed to go on forever, at least growing lighter as the sun started coming up far to the east, dimly lighting the dark entanglement of wood into a mosaic of a million shadows. Stone heard a sudden scream and stopped, turning around. He could see that one of them had fallen and was lying on the ground below, pierced through the side of his leg. The man just kept screaming, reeling this way and that, standing on one leg on the ground, the other pierced cleanly through by a stake. The recruits stared down dumbly, frozen above on different branches.

"Tie some belts together and pull him out. Someone strong ... like you, Bull," Stone screamed the fifty feet

through the thicket where he could dimly see the scene un-
folding. Bull at first glared at Stone but then thought better
about it and saw an opportunity for himself to be a hero. He
ripped his belt out from his pants, took three more from the
other men perched in his tree and attached them all together,
then lowered the homemade vine down to the bellowing
wounded man below.

"Take it, asshole," Bull screamed down, which even
Stone agreed was about the appropriate word for the situation. The screaming man calmed himself enough to grab
hold of the belt ladder and wrapped both of his arms firmly
around it. Bull leaned back against the base of the tree and
set both his legs up on branches ahead of him for leverage.
"Now hold on to this as strong as a scumbag around a har-
don," he yelled and started pulling. Luckily for both of them
the recruit who had fallen, one Doug "Badluck" Evans, all
the way from Montana, was light—with clothes on, around
one-fifty—whereas Bull weighed in at over two-fifty and
had the biceps to show it, not to mention the eyes of the rest
of the team focused on him, glowing, half-hidden in the
rolling darkness of this neo-jungle world.

Straining and cursing with every heave, Bull pulled the
man up one mighty take at a time. The veins in his neck
looked like they were going to explode and his cheeks grew
red as lobsters just thrown into the boiling pot, but he kept
pulling, hauling the man right up and off the stake, and up
into the tree. Arms reached out from nearby branches and
they jockeyed the wounded recruit onto the base of a thick
branch. But there was no way he could go forward—or
back. You could see into the bone through the puncture in
his leg. He'd have to stay. But that was his problem. They
tied him to the branch so he couldn't fall out if he lost

consciousness and then moved on ahead. They had their own problems.

Once they all got used to moving among the high branches, always being very cautious to make sure—after they had seen what happened to one who hadn't—that they had the next branch gripped firmly before they let go of the previous one, it wasn't so bad. It was even kind of fun in a way, if you could relax and forget that if you fell, a yard-long stake was going to go right through your face. Stone was far in the lead now, but those who followed behind could see the way by the broken branches he made as he moved along. And without admitting it to himself, he made the breaks a little bigger than necessary to make sure they could find them. They moved like this for hours, losing track of time in the sun-splattered streaks and beams that twisted down through the maze of branches.

At last, just as the sun was making its final ascent over far mountains, Stone came to a clearing and slid down the outermost tree. He waited a few seconds, staring back. The others were spread out in a long line behind, edging along. He didn't wait. Ahead was another trail that ran through a much thinner forest, little grooves of trees set among thigh-high brush. Stone moved ahead cautiously, his senses on full alert. God knew what they were planning for them next. As if in answer to his question, five men jumped out from the shadows of a copse of pines and came at him swinging staffs like the ones they had trained with the day before. Stone didn't falter an inch but headed right for the closest one. As the man came in with a circular overhead strike, Stone grabbed the end of the pole, pulled backwards with his whole body and fell down onto the ground. Digging the end he held into the dirt, he pulled the other end and the masked attacker right up into the air and overhead where he flew past, soaring about twelve feet before he crashed face first into the dirt. Continuing his backwards roll Stone came up with the staff in his hand just in time to block a slashing blow from another attacker. Stone didn't even pull his stick up but just pushed the end in his hands forward, aiming the other end for the groin. The stick poked the attacker's personal property and he went down as if hit by a rhino, writhing in pain on the ground.

Holding the staff in front of him, Stone ran through the ranks of attackers. Another came charging from the right and Stone caught the descending blow on the end of his stick and spun it back up with a flick of the wrist. The style he used in stick fighting was actually not what the NAA taught, but his father's personal style adapted from Japanese sword-fighting techniques—Iaido—that he had learned in the Pacific during World War II. But the effect was to turn the arm and striking implement of the opponent and then counter-strike with the speed and focus of a boxer. Stone snapped the pole back into the side of the attacker's head, almost dead on the temple, and the man fell like a rag doll and lay still in the dust. Stone hoped he hadn't killed him. He knew these were all part of the scenery. The next two backed off as he came at them with fire in his eyes, pole pulled back to the side, ready to strike. They darted back into the shadows and Stone let them go. Tucking the pole under his arm, he ran forward as fast as he could down a low hill.

From the yells and wood-slapping-flesh sounds behind him, Stone knew the others were being attacked, but that was their problem. His were what looked like quicksand pits ahead of him. The pathway narrowed into a sort of funnel, and the only way forward was through several hundred yards of thick mucky sand that looked like it could suck down a cow in seconds. Stone suddenly saw a series of rocks poking just out of the sand along both sides of the quicksand high-way and he started carefully along them. The going was immediately tough, since his boots kept slipping off and stepping into the slime. Stone stopped on two fairly good-sized rocks, and getting a good balance on one leg took off first one, then the other of his boots and the socks as well. He tentatively stepped forward with his bare feet. It was much better. The bare surface of his foot acted almost like a suction cup when it landed on the surface of each rock and became coated with the scummy surface layer. If anything, his feet became like suckers and were hard to pull off, releasing only with a loud sucking, almost sexual sound. But it made the quicksand crossing easy as he just set firmly down on one rock and then suctioned his foot to the next.

After about a half hour of this Stone emerged at the other end of the death trap and put his boots back on, then started forward, following the next red arrow pointing ahead. The direction led him down a long slowly sloping hill about a mile to a shoreline. But he had only come about a quarter mile when the image of some poor bastard going under the sand forever made him stop in his tracks. He turned and jogged back to the end of the pits. Sure enough, two men had fallen in about halfway along, one of them his foxhole sharer, Bo. The recruits behind them were frozen in place, unsure what to do.

Stone screamed across to them. "Take off your fucking shoes and socks, you bimbos. You can get traction with your feet." They tried it—and liked it. They quickly pulled out the two stranded ones and the entire group started across the shifting sands. Stone turned and headed back down the slope to the shore. After ten minutes he reached a sandy beach, the shore of a wide lake whose opposite side he could only dimly see far off. An arrow stood right by the lake, pointing into the water. Stone tried it with his foot, shivered and then started taking off his things. If he was going to have to swim through it he wanted to be as light as possible. He tied all his clothes into a ball, except for his pants. Stone tied the feet of these together, then lifted the thick cotton camouflage pants over his head, filling them with air. He quickly closed the waist end, sealing it tightly shut with his belt and then waded into the frigid waters holding the instant buoy, sealed with air so both of its cotton legs were filled out like balloons.

"Christ, it's cold," Stone screamed to the misting water surface. "I sure hope there's lifeboats and all that shit waiting for me out there, 'cause I already feel frozen like a fucking popsicle." He put the homemade preserver into the fairly flat surface of the lake and then settled down on top of it. It eased down into the black liquid but held his weight fine. Stone, his teeth chattering, praying the sun would rise soon and warm his half iced-over back, started paddling into the darkness. It wasn't that the journey itself was so difficult, but how cold it was that, he quickly realized, was going to be the problem. Stone swirled around slightly as he was caught in a light current and saw the first of the others coming onto the shore about a hundred yards off. They spotted his makeshift flotation device and pointed to him, yelling and laughing amongst themselves. Once again Stone had given them the way out of an apparently impossible situation.

Only thing was, Stone's arms and legs felt like they were tightening up by the second as he paddled across the ink-black lake. Below his feet he could feel little swirls of water from time to time and hoped it was nothing bigger than a breadbox that might take a bite out of him. But he knew he had to get across fast. His chest felt it was turning to cement, hardly able to breathe in the frigid air so tight were all the muscles in his body. When he discovered that he couldn't move his arms at all Stone just kept kicking forward, letting the hands steer in the water like a forward rudder.

It took forever but just as the sun rose like a lantern into the dark tree line on the shore, Stone made land, and gasping like a beached whale pulled himself up onto the sandy shore. And there, with a smile as big as a pumpkin's on Halloween, and a dark laugh to go with it, was Sergeant Zynishinski, staring at Stone like he was an insect from another galaxy.

CHAPTER
Fourteen

"RISE AND shine, Stone, the general wants to see you," a voice with the decibel level of an elephant in coitus interruptus bellowed into Stone's ear as he lay sprawled out on the cot of the recruit bunkhouse back inside the fortress walls. Stone tried to pull his head back under the covers, knowing it wasn't going to work.

"Come on, come on, Stone. You've slept eight hours, for Christ's sake. It's an honor for General Patton to want to see any raw recruit. He must have his eye on you. Now get that ass out of bed before I kick it out." Stone pulled the covers back and slowly peered out from between two half closed eyes.

"Why is that you are always waking me from what would be a perfect sleep if I could just get two hours more of it?"

"Mr. Stone, if sleep is what you crave," Sergeant Zynishinski said, releasing yet another immense gob of black and brown spit and chewing tobacco, "then you'd best desert fast and take your chances with the hound dogs. 'Cause you'll never get it here. Now get up. I'll be at the door. If you ain't there in two-and-a-half minutes, I'm breaking your head." He turned and stomped out, his size twelve EEE boots cracking down on the wooden barrack floor so that every half unconscious man twisted in his sleep. Stone rose and looked quickly around the place, counting—fifteen. So two more who had started the obstacle course hadn't made it through. He wondered who the poor bastards were and just what had happened to them. He dressed in the darkness and quickly headed toward the door, where he almost crashed straight on into the sergeant, who was coming back inside to get him.

"What happened to the other two?" Stone asked the D.I. as they walked quickly down the lane to the main thoroughfare.

"Quinn and Hartgast." The sergeant shook his head angrily. "Quinn took a strike to the throat during the staff attack. He may or may not make it. Hartgast never came out the other side of the lake. We keep an eye on everything. You can't see us but we were watching you all the whole way. If we can help it, no one dies. But the son-of-a-bitch seemed to be okay, then went under for a second . . . and never came up. This group was better than usual, actually," he commented. "We're lucky if we get ten or twelve make it all the way through. Seventeen this time. But a lot of that had to do with you, Stone. Like I say, I had my eye on you."

The sergeant led Stone toward a section of the fort he hadn't been in before, until they came to a three-story warehouse without a single window in the place. The whole thing was surrounded by a sandbagged and barbed-wired fence about ten feet high—almost creating a mini-fortress within the fort. A number of elite guards with the golden eagle clutching a skull on all their uniforms stood around, watching everything intently. Sergeant Zynishinski saluted and the two troopers by the door, these with Ingram submachine guns around their necks, let them through. Inside, Stone sucked in his breath—it was beautiful, filled with huge oil paintings on the walls, and plush persian carpets on the floor. Expensive antique furniture sat everywhere, dark wooden chairs and desks that looked as if they had all come from a museum.

"Yes," a lieutenant asked, looking up from a wide cherry desk just inside the outer door.

"General Patton specifically requested I bring this trooper to him first thing this morning." Sergeant Zynishinski said with a look of obvious distaste at the wimpy secretary. As far as the D.I. was concerned there was just two kinds of soldier—the fighting kind and all others. And he had a hard time relating to the "others." So he snorted hard and looked around for a place to spit out a black piece of slime-coated tobacco chew.

"Ah yes," the secretary said, taking a file card from a box in front of him. "Yes, the general was very anxious to see . . . Mr. Stone, is it?"

Stone nodded and smiled sweetly. He had done more smiling around this place than he had for the last five years. But then since he and his family—mom, dad and sister, megatypical American family—had spent most of the time fighting and yelling at one another, he hadn't had a lot of use for said expression. There was something about being trapped together inside a cave for five years—even a luxurious cave stocked with food and every amenity—that had brought out the nastiest parts of their personalities. The appointment secretary picked up a phone and pressed a button.

"Yes—Stone, sir. Send him right in? Thank you, sir." He hung the phone up gently, as if afraid to put it down too hard, and waved Stone through. Sergeant Zynishinski started along after him, but the secretary stopped him with an icy "Not you, Sergeant. Just Private Stone. You may leave. The general thanks you for your quick attention to his orders." The D.I. stared down at the shoulder-padded worm of a man with a look of tangible contempt. He had the strongest urge to take his head and slam it down on the perfect wax finish on the cherry desk beneath him. But he had been in the army too long to lose it all with such a violent impulsive motion. The sergeant had learned to push down his own emotions like one would kick an enemy in the face. Though it would be fun. He filled his barrel chest, stood up stiffly and turned on a dime toward the door.

"Couldn't have stayed anyway," the sergeant intoned clearly as he walked off. "Must attend to my men."

Stone gingerly pushed against two handcarved oak doors and they virtually flew open. And again his breath caught in his chest—it was . . . awesome. Huge oil paintings of Greek gods fighting among themselves in the heavens took up one wall; a picture of Napoleon, cracked and faded, clearly a masterpiece, took up another. Angels flying down from the sky on a third wall—hundreds of them with arched ivory wings, and the eyes of God himself staring from behind a cloud. Here and there around the large room suits of armor stood upright, as if guarding the art on the walls. And on the fourth wall, swords, ancient firearms, daggers hung everywhere, beautiful in their primitive lines and exaggerated antique features. Stone started slowly forward, hardly able to digest so much luxury, splendor—the gold candelabra in the ceiling, the black velvet couches on the sides of the rooms, the library of gilded books that rose floor to ceiling in the corner, the Greek vases and Chinese porcelains . . .

"Ah, Private Stone," a voice said from his side. Stone turned to see a powerful-looking man seated in a leather armchair. It was Patton—unmistakable. Stone had seen his picture enough on the walls of the main buildings. Next to the NAA flag it was the most repeated image. But in person, the general looked much more vibrant, alive, with piercing crystal-blue eyes that seemed as if they could burn right through you. Stone almost instinctively saluted, instantly feeling angry at himself for playing soldier boy so well. But Patton looked pleased and motioned for him to sit.

"Please, please, take a seat. Have a cup of coffee." He pointed toward a steaming electric brewer on a small table to the side. "It's my own mixture, made from a number of different beans we have in the warehouse." Stone leaned over and poured a cup, then sat in the chair. It seemed to fit his body perfectly and Stone wondered for a second if the arms were going to spring up and grab him. He quickly lifted the cup to his lips and took a sip. It was delicious, the best coffee he'd had since going into the bunker, where it had been all frozen and instant and almost undrinkable after the first year.

"Excellent," Stone said, his mouth still glued to the edge of the cup. He took another gulp. The high caffeine content flowed instantly into his veins and Stone felt his eyes open wide and his mind suddenly snap into second gear.

"It's beautiful, isn't it?" the general asked as he swept his hand around the room.

"It's incredible, General," Stone said, letting his eyes make a more careful sweep this time. Still, there was too much to even begin to comprehend, just a blur of art and military objects that belonged more in a king's castle or a

Rockefeller's Hudson River mansion than in a windowless, rust-tinged warehouse in the middle of nowhere. "I've never seen so much," he struggled for the words, "expensive-looking furnishing anywhere . . . and in my time I've seen some high level places."

"Yes, I love beautiful things," the general said, rising from his chair and starting to pace around the room. He reached out and stroked the art objects as if they were alive, running his hands across the surfaces of Rembrandts and Michelangelos, along the spine of a statue of a horse. Stone studied the general carefully. He was a big broad-shouldered man with a military bearing much like his father's; around his hips sat two ivory-handled .45's, which, if Stone remembered, the World War II Patton had adorned himself with too. A McArthur-style jutting jaw and weather-burned skin, lines around the eyes, the cheeks grooved. The face of someone who had been out in the world all his life instead of hiding from it. But it was those eyes—those laser eyes that looked as if they saw through everything—like the major's. So many things about General Patton reminded Stone of his father that it unnerved him; it threatened to bring up unresolved conflicts with the old man that he hardly needed to pyschotheraphize right now.

"Beauty is what makes it all worth fighting for, Stone," General Patton went on, walking around the room, stroking his prize possessions.

"Indeed." Stone coughed, unsure what to say about such a statement. He hadn't seen too much beauty lately.

"I need men who appreciate beauty—and who *want* it, Stone," Genreal Patton said, suddenly turning and glueing Stone to the chair with those ice pick eyes. Stone just dug his face a little deeper into the coffee, having no idea what the general was getting at.

"You did well on your training, Stone. Excellently in fact. From what Sergeant Zynishinski has relayed to me, you displayed not just ingenuity in getting through the obstacle course, but went out of your way to provide leadership to the rest of the recruits. In fact, I was informed that several more lives might have been lost but for your intervention. Excellent, excellent, Stone. I need men who can think on their feet. Men who can dare to rise above the herd. I have many recruits, more and more every day now. But you see what most of them are like—half of them dumb cows from the caves, the rest morons from the mountains. And most of those who make it through are useless as anything more than cannon fodder. I need men who can be leaders, Stone. Men like you."

"That's—uh—great," Stone said, lifting his head from the cup. He reached forward and poured himself another cup. It might be a long time before he'd have coffee like this again. The general came back over and sat down across from Stone with an intent look on his craggy face. He swept his hand back through his slicked-back gray-silver hair and looked at Stone with a fanatical intensity in those missile eyes.

"We're moving, Stone. God, are we moving. It's taken me five years to get to this point—to finally have the trained men and the firepower I need to support them. And now I do. But you know what I don't have, Stone?" The general didn't wait for the answer but leaned forward. "I don't have the son-of-a-bitches to take those fighting soldiers out there and do some heavy-duty cleanup of the whole damned central part of our country. We could take back twenty, thirty miles a day if I had the right staff."

"That seems fairly ambitious, General," Stone said,

knowing the terrain for hundreds of miles around to be some of the roughest in the nation.

"No, Mr. Stone, it's not ambitious, it's a fact," Patton said confidently, walking over to the library of fine books in the far corner. "You know what it is that really separates me from the savages and the warlords out there, Stone?" Patton didn't wait for an answer and Stone didn't try to give one. "This"—he pulled a leather-bound book from a shelf and held it out in the air. "Knowledge, Stone. History. The history of warfare—*that* makes the difference, and nothing else. Two things, Stone, above all else—speed and armor. 'Blitzkrieg und Panzer,' as they used to say. All my offensive strategic planning has centered around the concept of the fast mobile strike using tanks and wheel-mounted artillery. And that we have here, Stone. Twenty Bradley III tanks with 120mm cannon and .30 and .50 machine guns on front and back. A dozen jeeps and trucks pulling 155mm howitzers with 20 foot barrel. Firepower, that's what it all comes down to ultimately, Stone, the ability to send down punishing waves of shells on the enemy. To grind him to a pulp. As both my illustrious namesake, General George S. Patton and his wartime nemesis, Rommel, proved: with the right firepower—primarily tanks—in the right place at the right time, a man can do just about anything. The tank is and always will be the most lethal, unstoppable land weapon man has ever created."

Patton stopped, put his hand to his chest and sat back down in his chair, knowing he had to relax, that his blood pressure was rising again. He took his pulse and waited until it seemed to have slowed down.

"Can't let myself die now, can I?" he asked Stone with a quick smile. "Who'd run this whole goddamned show?" Stone grinned back. He liked the guy. There was a tremendous sense of power, of almost pure electricity about the man. Stone had never met anyone with so much personal charisma before except perhaps his old man. He could see why the general could get his men to fight for him, could keep the whole damned army together with just the force of his personality. For the fire that burned inside his eyes was the flame of genius, and even the dumbest man who looked could see that it was so.

A dog suddenly pushed through a side door and Stone nearly did a double take. It was Excaliber . . . how the hell could . . . ? But as the dog walked with the total assurance that was the mark of the breed across the Persian rugs that covered the floor, Stone saw that, though remarkably similar, the animal had different coloration and was slightly smaller than his own fighting terrier. The pitbull walked up to Patton and pushed his head against the general's leather boots.

"Yes, Hannibal, good dog," the general said as he scratched the pitbull on the head. "Beautiful animal, isn't he?" Patton said, looking up at Stone. "He's a pitbull and—"

"Yes, I know the species," Stone answered. "I happen to have one of my own. He was rescued along with me, and is in your animal warehouse right now."

"Why, that's amazing," the general commented as he pushed the dog's jaws away from his black leather boots, which the animal had started to half-heartedly chew on. "You are an unusual catch, aren't you. Perhaps we could have a little match between the two of them. Not to the death, of course, but . . . just to see which is the fiercer, which the stronger bloodline."

"I don't think so, General," Stone said, remembering the last time he had had to make the pitbull fight—against an immense Doberman. It had been a bloody experience. "Although he travels with me, he's his own dog. I don't make him do anything he basically doesn't want to. And arranging a match, I'm afraid, would fall into that category."

"A shame," Patton said, clapping his hands loudly. The pitbull turned sharply and headed back out the door. "Perhaps you—or your dog—will have a change of heart. It would be a most interesting diversion."

"I'll have a little talk with him, and see what kind of mood he's in," Stone said with a half grin.

"Stone . . . Martin Stone," Patton said softly, looking at a file card. He had put reading glasses on but half hid them from Stone as if he didn't want the younger man to see that the supreme commander had any deficiencies whatsoever. "Tell me, it's extremely unlikely, but are you by any chance related to Clayton Stone? Major Clayton R. Stone." Stone gulped down hard the final lukewarm swig of coffee from the cup.

"Yes. I'm hi—his son." He coughed, some of the grounds from the bottom of the cup getting stuck in his throat.

"I'll be damned," General Patton said, pounding his fist into the palm of the other hand. "I knew your old man well. We were in Vietnam together. The son-of-a-bitch was actually theoretically under me at one point, but he just evaded my chain of command and went off and did his own thing. He was something else. A genius at what he did. You know, don't you, that his long range reconnaissance patrols, in which he went all the way into northern 'Nam and left trails of heads in the forests, are famous throughout Asia—infamous, I should say. There's never been anyone better."

He stared hard at Stone. "I've made my mind up. Everything about you clicks together. I have no time, Stone, to play around. I've got to move now. There's just no time. If my

plans came together I could strike a blow that would change
the course of America. I'm going to take a chance on you
and do something that I've never done before. If you succeed, the sky is the limit. Those who join me now will be
powerful men in five years. You could have this all, and
more, Stone."

In spite of himself, Stone found his brain permeated by
the messianic, almost hypnotic energy with which the general spoke. It wouldn't be so bad having some of these
things, Stone thought, hardly ever having been so impressed
in his life with sheer objects. He felt seduced by it all.

"What—what is it that you want me to do?" Stone asked
hesitantly, knowing that the last thing you were supposed to
do in the army was volunteer.

"There's a band of mountain bandits about thirty miles
from here. They've been preying on passing caravans and
even families. They're scum, Stone. Scum of the worst kind
—mutilating, raping, taking the organs of the dead to cook
back in their camps. The kind of lice that must be wiped out
so that we can clear the way for decent, civilized people. I
want you to lead the strike force against them. Tomorrow,
take them into the mountains and destroy this cancer. And if
you succeed"—he looked at Stone with those laser pupils—
"If you succeed, it is obvious what will happen. You can
take what you want, Stone."

Martin was strangely moved by the general's words. The
fact that such a brilliant military mind, a man who hardly
knew him, had come to trust him so much so quickly filled
Stone with a flushed pride. His ego swelled up like a sponge
from the attention. He looked over at the Michelangelo on
the wall. Imagine that in the bunker. It would be like some
sort of mad monument to his father. Just to show him something that Stone had never been able to express in life. And

now in death couldn't. But maybe his spirit would see, would feel the presence of such a masterpiece.

"Anything?" Stone asked.

"Anything," Patton said coolly.

"Then let's do it one by one. I'll carry out *this* battle assignment for . . . *that*." He pointed toward the wall, toward the Michelangelo teeming with angels, flying down from the cloud-dappled face of God himself. Stone thought he might have insulted the general but instead the man instantly began laughing and reached out to slap Stone on the back.

"Absolutely. My gift to you, Mr. Stone, upon the successful completion of your mission. I like a man who knows just what he wants—and dares to take it. Then I always know what his motivation is."

"That and my dog, Excaliber, who's in your pens. And finally, the use of my Harley, which has been impounded since I've been here."

"I'm not used to being given demands," Patton said, rising again and pacing nervously. "But in your case I'll excuse it, because it is yet another proof to me that you are a wolf, not a sheep. Yes, you can have it all. There is plenty more where this came from." He threw a casual glance at the immense work of art that seemed almost alive, so filled was it with motion and swirling supernatural creatures.

"So you accept the assignment, Stone," Patton asked.

"Yes sir, I do," Stone said. "It will be my pleasure to take out the bastards who've been terrorizing the area. I've run into that kind of slime all over the place and I always thought it was a shame there wasn't an organized force to go after them—get rid of them once and for all. It would be an honor to contribute to such a venture."

"Good, then it's settled. You'll leave this afternoon, to command a hundred-man force with appropriate mobile ar-

tillery." He reached down and opened the drawer of a ma-
hogany desk, took out a few items and turned back toward
Stone. "But I can't allow a private to lead a force of that
size. This *is* the army after all. Here." He handed Stone one
of the golden eagles with skull—and the marks of a full
colonel.

"The men aren't going to like this," Stone said to the
general as he hesitantly pinned the eagle to his collar and the
stripes to his shoulders.

"I don't give a damn what any man thinks," Patton half
bellowed. "I make the decisions around here. And anyone
who ever forgets it will find himself in front of a firing
squad that night. That goes for you too, Stone. I'm putting a
lot of faith in you." For the first time that morning the leader
of the Third Army looked angry for a moment. And Stone
could see that inside those eyes there was a darkness, a black
curtain behind the shimmering blue surface. Something that
hinted at unspeakable deeds. But Martin Stone, in the midst
of being offered more power than he'd ever held in his life,
was blind to the flaws.

CHAPTER
Fifteen

THREE TANKS sped across the canyon country to the east of Grand Junction where Fort Bradley was located. They moved fast, and low to the ground, the super-mobile Bradley III being a far more successful model than its predecessors. Four troop trucks came lumbering behind them like beasts of burden, three filled with NAA troops—battle-hardened men, some of the toughest under General Patton's command—the fourth with heavy combat weapons including .50 caliber machine guns, mortars, even a few flamethrowers. A 150mm howitzer was linked up to the rear truck and its long barrel arched like a spear. A cloud of dust rose behind them, hanging in the afternoon air about fifty feet off the ground as it was an almost windless day.

The terrain around them was stark, almost primeval in its appearance. This was some of the most mountainous and barren territory in Colorado: hard, almost lifeless, ground beneath the tire treads of their whining vehicles, towering red sandstone sculptures rising all around them, carved by the ceaseless wind of the ages into shapes of mushrooms, lions, pyramids. You could see anything if you looked long enough.

But Stone was more interested in the mechanical workings of the tank he was in than the tortured beauty outside. He sat in the codriver's seat next to the tank commander and watched intently his every move. It was a fairly simple steering mechanism, using two bars that controlled each tread system separately. It enabled the driver to turn on a dime or, by pushing both all the way forward or pulling them all the way back, to accelerate to thirty-five mph within six seconds, from full speed to a skidding stop within forty feet. Stone kept asking questions over and over, wanting to cement the knowledge of every bit of the tank's workings in his brain. The driver—Lieutenant Carpenter—pointed each button and dial out.

"Now, the gunner can operate the turret separately," Carpenter said to Stone as he stared into a video monitor that showed the rushing landscape outside. Stone glanced around at the gunner, who sat off to the right side of the large control chamber, with earphones on that connected him to every other man in the crew and goggles that gave him as well a video picture of the world outside. He constantly fiddled with dials on it so the armored camera swept three hundred and sixty degrees around the tank, searching for trouble. "Or the driver of the Bradley can operate every system from up here." He swept his hand over the digital display panel that ran in front of them across the entire eight-foot width of the tank.

It was a five man crew, which, with Stone as a sixth, made it a tight squeeze. But as Lieutenant Carpenter was telling him, the other five men were actually redundant. In reality the driver alone could not only drive the tank, but could fire its 120mm cannon, its .30 and .50 caliber machine guns, send off any or all of its eight radar-controlled ground-to-ground mini-missiles capable of taking out a tank twice the Bradley's relatively compact thirty-foot length. And do a couple of other things as well.

"And this—if everything else fails," Lt. Carpenter said with a sardonic grin as he glanced over at Stone, "is the self-destruct timer. The general doesn't want any of our equipment—certainly not a Bradley—to get into the hands of the enemy. So you just crack open the glass here," he mock-demonstrated with a small red hammer attached to the encased timer by a chain. "And set the clock inside by turning to the right. Then flick the Arm lever—it's here. And then run. 'Cause every ounce of explosive in the tank— every shell, every bit of fuel—will all go at once. Anyone inside will be barbecued to a char. Even the vultures wouldn't be able to eat their black ashes."

"Sounds great," Stone said. "I'll keep it in mind for whenever I'm feeling suicidal. Tell me, do you think I could drive it a little; I want to learn. If I'm in command of a whole damn tank force I'd sure as hell better know how to even get the thing going." The lieutenant hesitated just a second as the rest of the crew's ears perked up. Stone had met with less animosity than he had thought he would—being promoted to full colonel, given command of such a formidable strike force out of nowhere. But the rest of the operation, including the assorted captains and majors who rode in the other tanks and in two officers' jeeps to the rear, had not expressed any hostility to Stone. Whatever they felt, he was in the game now, a protegé of Patton. His powers might soon be immense. And so none of them would risk his displeasure. They expressed neither friendliness nor malevolence, just a cool noncommittal attitude that said: "Let's see just how long you last, sucker."

"Sure, I guess it will be all right," the lieutenant said after a few seconds. "I mean, you're the guy running the damned show."

"Just keep an eye on me, okay?" Stone asked with a sheepish look. He didn't want to crash the thing right into the side of one of the sandstone spires. That would be a great way to start a mission, blowing up his vehicle. Stone still couldn't really belive the whole thing was happening. And he wasn't quite sure that he had the faintest idea what a colonel was supposed to do.

"I'll grab them away," the lieutenant said, sitting back so Stone could slide over in front of the steering bars, "if anything starts going wrong." Stone took hold of the bars and stared into the slightly wavering monitor above him on the instrument panel. The road ahead looked peculiar, as if he were watching a rerun instead of reality, but in a few seconds his eyes adjusted to the level of the video light. It was actually all very easy. The bars were sensitive to the motion of his arms so Stone hardly had to move at all to steer. He would slow it down a little, then speed it up, twisting back and forth slightly, trying to get the feel.

"What happens if the TV goes on the blink?" Stone asked.

"As I explained earlier," Carpenter said in an almost bored monotone, "everything has a backup. You just slide back that bolt and the shielding comes down on hinges. The other side contains a two-inch-thick super resin Fiberglas window through which you can view ahead."

"Who's driving that damned lead tank?" A voice suddenly burst onto their headphones. "This is Colonel Malik. My driver informs me that you're weaving all over the damned place."

"This is Colonel Stone," Stone said like ice through his mouthpiece. "I'm at the controls here. Why, is there a problem?"

"Oh, no problem, sir," the voice apologized. "Sorry, didn't realize."

"Carry on, Colonel," Stone said, suddenly appreciating the fringe benefits of power. They drove through the afternoon and into the evening, and still went on. With the infrared and other light-enhancing visual capabilities of the video system one could see as clearly as if it were daylight. Stone and Lieutenant Carpenter took shifts of an hour each as the concentration level of driving the high-tech Bradley was extremely intense. The tank even had a coffee machine that the crew kept loading up. After the fifth cup of the foul-tasting but highly caffeinated brew, Stone felt like his eyeballs were popping out of his head. But it gave him and the other men energy to drive on through the darkness. Sergeant Zynishinski had been right: if he wanted to get sleep the New American Army was not going to be the place to do it.

The fleet drove through the darkness. Around them canyons and ripped broken strips of land, bizzare sandstone formations, all shimmering with the scalpel rays of the half-moon, glowing as if they were alive. Stone only had one mishap, misjudging a small rise and letting the tank go over it at forty mph. The right tread lifted up high and fast, and suddenly the entire tank was almost over at a forty-five degree angle. Every man in the crew looked as if a jolt of electricity had just gone through them as adrenaline surged into their veins. But just as quickly the tank slammed back down again—creating a funnel of dust all around it—and kept going like nothing had happened.

After several hours they hit a plateau that looked across a

vast jigsaw puzzle of low mountains, woods and rock canyons.

"We stop here!" Stone commanded over the headphones as he brought the tank to a smooth halt and handed back controls of the Bradley to Carpenter, who took the operating seat with something approaching relief in his bloodshot eyes. Stone exited the tank and walked to the very edge of the plateau, where he lifted a pair of field glasses and scanned the hard terrain that spread off to the horizon. A bloated orange sun with a somewhat sickly look dragged itself above the far mountains, spitting out just enough light for Stone to pick up a few details in the gray morning mists that swept across the death lands. Far off—miles away—he thought for a second that he saw a fire—several of them, burning hard—but then more fog moved in and the view was obscured.

The other officers came up alongside him—a total of eight for this mission—and one of them, Colonel Garwood, coughed and tried to catch his attention. He had had a run-in with Garwood before, but Stone wouldn't hold it against him. He wasn't going to be an asshole about the officer thing.

"Colonel Stone, if I may be so presumptuous," Colonel Garwood said, standing just behind him. Stone turned, lowering the glasses. "We thought we might suggest a strategy meeting at this point." The colonel spoke with polite, even tones but Stone knew that the bastard hated him. *He* would have been the one leading the strike except for Stone. And Stone knew also that they were all keeping a close eye on him. Patton wanted to test him at many levels at once. They were waiting, searching for the slightest weakenss, the smallest fatal error. And then they would pounce, like hyenas on the kill of a lion. Too cowardly to attack themselves, they would wait to feed from the prey once it had been already wounded.

"Yes . . . I was just going to call one," Stone replied. The tension between him and the officers was almost palpable. He just prayed that none of them had the balls to shoot him in the back. The troops from the transport had already exited and were setting up a momentary camp, awaiting orders from their superiors. A folding table was quickly set up for the officer corps, and maps were unfolded on it.

"Here," Colonel Garwood said, pointing to a spot on the smudged map, which had obviously been used numerous times before. "Our latest intelligence is that the main camp of the bandits is here."

"How old is that intelligence report?" Stone asked.

"One month, perhaps two at most," the colonel replied indignantly, as if almost insulted by the question.

"Then I want more up-to-date info before we mount an attack," Stone said, letting his eyes meet every officer's there. Now was the time to exert authority, to show them that whatever they thought of him he was going to be the boss. "We'll have to do reconnaissance. Send out scouts."

"We have a team of highly trained forward intell—" Garwood began. But Stone cut him off in mid-sentence.

"I'll go!" Stone said simply. "I always do my own recon before I attack." The others sputtered and looked incredulous.

"But the commanding officer of a search-and-destroy mission NEVER goes forward himself," Garwood said angrily. "It would be an abrogation of responsibility of the highest order. Possibly subject to court-martial proceedings."

"Nonetheless, I'm going. Going now," Stone said firmly. "We shouldn't send a force this large into that kind of terrain—open to ambush from every quarter—unless we know exactly what's in store. I take the lives of the men in this unit seriously. That's why I'm going to be careful—very careful."

"You are in command, of course," Garwood said, again flashing that shining smile that made Stone want to check his back to make sure it hadn't been stabbed. "But we will have to insist that several men accompany you—if only for your protection." Stone knew they just wanted to keep an eye on him. He had nothing to hide.

"If they don't get in my way, they can come." He looked down at his NAA-issue watch. "Five minutes, then I leave." He rose from the table and went to pick up a few things he needed for the reconnaissance. The officers stared after him with contempt. The man wasn't an officer. Officers did things a certain way. There were many things to consider. There had to be a minimum number of strategy meetings, discussions about the best way to proceed. Only Stone was the get-up-and-do-it type. And it drove the rule and regulated brass half crazy as if he were challenging the very foundations on which their lives were based.

Two huge fellows decked out light with just submachine guns and binocs came up to Stone and saluted with their fists in front of their eyes.

Stone returned the salute in a perfunctory manner.

"Sir, we're the forward scouts you requested. I'm Corporal Jenkins, this is Corporal Powers. We're both from these parts; that's why they use us." Stone looked them over quickly. They looked all right, a little more unkempt than the average NAA soldier, with stubble on chins, guns used and faded, with the look a weapon gets when it's killed a number of men.

"I move fast," Stone said, looking at both of them, staring into their eyes, to make sure they weren't assassins out to liquidate him. "No stopping for breath, no taking out maps to figure out where we are. No bullshit. Okay?"

"Okay sir." Both positively smiled back. It was the way they went too. And in the youthful and even enthusiastic faces, Stone felt suddenly confident that he could find no traces of murder directed at him.

"Then let's go. Just stay behind me." He slid over the side of the plateau and moved like a skidding stone down the steep slope. The two scouts jumped as well, and followed one after another. Within seconds they could see that they were going to have to put out all their energy just to keep up with the man. Stone moved down the slope at full speed. He wanted to be down lower when the sun lit up the pebble-and-rock-strewn mountainside. For all he knew there were scouts sent out by the enemy too. They could be making binocular sweeps just as he had. If Stone had learned one thing so far, it was to never underestimate even the most apparently barbaric and filth-coated of the killer bands out there. They were like rats—smart, tough as blood-stained steel.

He hit the bottom of the mountain upon which the rest of the force was bivouaced and started instantly across the lunar landscape ahead. The ground was hard as coal and sharp, with what appeared to be earthquake-created fissures every thirty or forty yards, and chasms in the granite that appeared to have no bottom. But after about an hour of it he at last reached the far side, where a series of pine-covered rocky canyons began. Stone glanced around behind him and saw the scouts clambering along the edges of the chasms, but he didn't wait.

He headed through the twisted rock valleys toward the fires he had spotted earlier with the glasses. And his sense of direction was unerring, for soon he smelled traces of smoke on the wind. He slowed down, edging up through a grove of pines that stood on the top of a rise and froze in mid-motion. He was right over them, looking down onto the camp of the bandits. There were about a dozen ramshackle buildings built of wood with tin roofing, none of them very straight or nailed into place quite right. And around the camp men strolled, performing various tasks. They were a wretched-looking lot. As bad as Stone had seen—with faces out of a nightmare, filled with scars and boils and pus-dripping sores that the bandits didn't even bother to clean. He lowered the binocs and saw that they were stepping in their own excrement, piles of shit that lay everywhere. You couldn't get much lower, Stone thought to himself as he lay flat just inside the cover of the trees. They were about fifty feet below him in the center of a canyon, the floor of which was about a hundred feet wide and five hundred long.

Then he saw that you could get lower as he focused the binoculars again. Half butchered bodies came into view, strung out on a long high pole. Over a dozen of them. Men, women, it was hard to even tell anymore as these had no heads, some of them no arms or legs. The gourmet etiquette of the meat eaters obviously allowed them to just go up and hack off a piece and hold it over the fire for a minute or two, just enough to get that golden brown sizzle. And as he watched, one of them hungry for lunch came over and did just that, sawing off a foot of one of the blood drained corpses and sticking it on the end of a branch. It splattered grease onto the flames and they popped up in little exploding bubbles. Then after a minute he pulled it off and began chewing away at it—toes first—spitting out the bones.

Stone was afraid he might puke, especially as the smell of the burning rotted flesh came up on a draft and hit him full in the nostrils. It was a smell he would not soon forget. He made a complete scan of the encampment and then went back over it again, searching out weapons stacks, where the main barracks were, everything he would need to know to formulate his battle plan. More hungry bandits emerged from a long wooden building and headed for the gutted corpses dangling in the wind. But Stone let the glasses fall around his chest. He'd seen enough.

He had started back down the outer slope of the valley wall when he saw just at the periphery of his vision a shape suddenly launch itself from the branches of a tree above him. But the added quarter second of warning gave him enough time to take a blow from a boot on the side of his shoulder rather than his head. He fell down, letting his body go limp, and as he hit the ground, rolled away from the attacker. He rose and shook his shoulder, which felt like it had rivulets of fire streaming through it. His attacker was rising too from the shadows at the base of the thick trees. A bandit—wild eyes, long black beard filled with garbage that had accumulated in it, the whole side of his face eaten away, probably from radiation, Stone thought, wincing as he saw it. For the flesh was missing down to the bone and on one side of its face it almost appeared that the mountain killer was just a fleshless skull.

Stone pulled a blade from his boot and rushed the man, trying to reach him before he regained his balance. But the bastard was quick, like a mountain cat, twisting and snarling. The grease-covered lips moved wildly, screaming in hate and fear as Stone charged, but no sounds came out. Stone's luck—the attacker was mute, probably from the radiation. If he could just kill the pretty boy without making a sound, he might be able to avoid the camp being alerted. The attacker pulled out a dulled butcher knife from within his blood-streaked robe, tailored from what looked like a woman's winter coat, and pulled it back to stab him.

Why everyone pulled back their knives was beyond
Stone. He stepped inside, blocked with the left hand and
plunged his blade into the bandit's throat. It went in on the
right side just below the jawline and Stone pulled it hard
across the front, cutting the Adam's apple, cutting everything in its path. He ripped the blade free when he reached
the other side and stepped back. A torrent of blood exploded
out of the slit throat, as if everything inside the man were
trying to bubble out at once. Gurgling a horrible fishlike
sound, the thing sank to the ground and grew quickly still,
though his blood continued to pump for ten minutes before
the heart sputtered to a halt.

Stone heard a branch crack and turned with the red blade
held out in front of him. But it was just the two NAA scouts,
finally having caught up with him. They stared down at the
twitching body and the blade in Stone's hand. The man was
tough. The rumors they had heard through the grapevine
were true. They looked at him with a new respect, which
Stone saw and ignored with a snort of disgust. He never
wanted to be admired for killing. It came too easy to him.

"Help me hide him," Stone said curtly and the three of
them dragged the nearly dead slab of flesh to a gulley, where
they covered it with leaves. Stone sprinkled more of the
brown leaves and some dirt over the trail of blood until it
seemed hidden. "Let's get the fuck out of here," he said to
the scouts, who looked a little disappointed. Somehow they
had missed all the action.

CHAPTER
Sixteen

BACK AT the waiting NAA strike force, Stone huddled with the officer corps inside a tent as the afternoon fell to evening and the purple sky brought in a frigid wind, reminding them that it was, after all, winter, and that nature would do whatever the fuck she felt like, whenever she felt like it. Stone was content to basically let them plan the format of the attack. Patton's tank strategy would, as always, be used. They would surround the canyon hideout with the four Bradleys and the wheel-mounted 155mm howitzer. Stone had seen relatively slow angled slopes at different sides of the mountains that surrounded the bandits, so the battlewagons should be able to get into position.

Stone let them feel as if *they* were planning the operation; he wasn't an idiot. He knew they had to feel they were running the show, or they would be resistant, play games with him. Stone was content to watch it all. They, after all, were the "experts" at large-scale armored warfare. He added only one plan to the entire operation, the sending of the infantry first to seal the bandits in—in case the tanks were heard before they had a chance to open up with cannon. And thus Operation Bandit Sweep IV—the fourth time they'd tried to take on this particular group of flesh-eating slime— was set in motion.

They waited until the sun slid into the coalpit of the evening and the magnetic curtains of the aurora borealis began to wave and whip high above the earth to the far north. The strike force broke up into four units, each with a tank in the lead and infantry surrounding them, and headed off the plateau in different directions. They had to take a far more circuitous route than Stone had, onto slopes slow enough for the tanks' treads to be able to grip. But if the maps held up, they would all be able to pick out a zigzagging trail and get there. Stone let Lieutenant Carpenter drive the Bradley. Here, in such tight quarters—boulders, trees all around them—he didn't want to take a chance. At lower speed, with additional muffler equipment thrown into operation, the tanks were only about a quarter of the volume of their normal noise level. The bandits would hear them at a half mile or less. But by then—or so the plan went—it would be too late.

It took Stone's tank half the night to complete the wide route to their slope, the southern approach, but at last the lieutenant pulled the Bradley to a stop about a mile from the almost circular wall of tree-dotted slopes that surrounded the bandit camp. Stone looked at his watch in the luminous green lights that filled the inside of the tank. Four-thirty exactly. They were right on schedule.

"Now, you know the plan, right?" Stone asked as he rose

and started up the metal-runged ladder that led to the exit hatch.

"Infantry gets in place. Five hundred we start moving; will proceed to coordinates A-14, K-27 and commence firing on enemy."

"Sounds right," Stone said. "Good luck," he added a little too stiffly, and then was gone up the ladder. He still had no idea quite how this commander stuff really worked and wondered for the fiftieth time if he really had a career cut out for him in the NAA. Stone took command of the twenty-five troops who were milling around in the front of the tank, waiting. It was still dark, the sky devoid of moon or magnetic stripes or anything. It was that dead time of the morning when night had vanished without a trace but morning hadn't really arrived on the scene yet. It is death's favorite time, the hour when most men die.

Stone led the force across the rocky terrain and then up the brush-covered slope. It was only a few minutes to the top and then they set themselves around the edge of the rise, staring down onto the bandit stronghold. If the slime had any idea that something was up they were sure pretending good. Spirals of smoke drifted up from the long huts, while five men attended a large bonfire in the center of the camp that they always seemed to keep going, throwing branches on from time to time. Stone checked his watch again by the first weak rays of the sun that drifted through the mountain mists to the east. He was into his second day without sleep. Already the NAA training was paying off. It was five o'clock —the tanks should be moving in. Stone heard the distant rumblings of the Bradleys, which grew louder by the second.

Suddenly the bandits were stirring. Lanterns snapped on inside two of the wooden structures and within seconds

naked and half naked men came running out with rifles in
their hands. The infantry forces had been ordered to hold
their fire until the shit actually hit the fan. But it clearly had.
Stone opened up along with the rest of them, firing the
M-16, which bucked in his hands like something alive.

The rest of the infantry forces had apparently gotten into
place on all four sides, for sparks of lights lit up the darkness
around the upper edge of the valley slopes as round after
round descended into the encampment. The first rush of
mountain men from the doorways was cut to ribbons, suddenly dancing an insane jig of jerking arms and legs, spewing blood out in a red whirlwind as their bodies were spun
around by the sheer intensity of the fire. The bandits re-
treated back into their half caved-in wood buildings and various little trenches they had dug throughout the camp.
Several machine guns opened up from camouflaged ditches
in the ground and Stone saw a line of slugs dig into the slope
below him, jackhammering the loose rocks there into
powder that filled the air with acrid dust for a few seconds
before settling down. So it was going to be a battle after all.
These flesh-eating son-of-a-bitches weren't going to give it
up easily.

Suddenly the tank was there, coming up the pebble-cov-
ered slope just behind him, treads digging furiously into the
loose gravellike surface, spitting out an arch of the stuff
behind them. But the steel teeth of the Bradley found traction enough to grind its way forward until it was settled in
between Stone and his men, high up on the canyon wall.
The immense 120mm cannon, which seemed almost over-
sized on the relatively small frame, swiveled around and
down until it had one of the larger cabins in its sights. Stone
covered his ears and the entire vehicle shook violently as a
sheet of flame roared out the front of the cannon. The cabin

was suddenly a rising ball of flame and smoke and twisting timbers spinning crazily like pick-up sticks through the air. And within it, Stone could see bloody puppetlike things, their arms and legs twisting and flopping around at impossible angles.

Two more of the tanks had found their range and let off bursts of brilliant fire from across the canyon. The structure next to the first, pieces of which were just starting to fall in smoking meteoric trails back down to earth, also went up in a ball of red and white, with such volume that Stone couldn't even hear the screams that started issuing forth from below. The tanks opened up with everything they had, shooting down shell after shell until the entire center of the encampment was ablaze and smoking. It was a bloodbath, a blazing burial ground for everyone caught in the cross fire below.

After five minutes of the unceasing barrage, the tanks and infantry stopped firing. The air was punctuated with numerous screams of the wounded below and the crackling of the many fires that burned everywhere. Stone looked through his field glasses and suddenly saw a white flag being waved from what looked like a solid piece of ground. An arm followed and the flag waved higher as a door opened in the dirt toward the far side of the canyon floor. A woman emerged with a look of terror on her face, then another, and a child. Within a few seconds there were several dozen of them, women and infants, half clothed, covered with dirt. They looked pitiful, about the saddest state to which Stone had ever seen the human species sink. Still, they were human—and women and children.

He turned to give the order for a team to go down and take them prisoner when the tank behind him opened up again. Stone was almost knocked from his feet by the blast, which went off only yards from his ear. He shook himself from the effects and couldn't believe his eyes. All the tanks had opened up, along with the infantry, pouring a stream of shell and slugs into the unarmed wretched refuse of the camp. Stone screamed, "No, no!" waving his hands at the tank, at where he knew the video camera could see him. But it was already too late. Two cannon shells landed dead center of the crying and sniveling group. Their flesh was blasted into paste, their bones into a million little pieces of shrapnel that flew out in all directions. When the smoke had cleared, there was nothing to be seen, except, lying almost untouched, the head of one of the children, which had been severed cleanly from its body. It sat in a smoking crater, dead center of it, like some sort of idol to death, a symbol of the unspeakable violence that firepower could do to human flesh.

Stone watched speechless, numb. As the other soldiers cheered all around him, flamethrower units came pouring down all four sides of the inner canyon walls, two men to a unit. They joined up at one end and formed a line about thirty feet apart. Then they ignited their long gas-spewing wands, and four tongues of swirling red fire spat out sixty feet ahead of them. Side by side they walked along the canyon floor, burning everything in front of them. Burning the cabins, and the bodies that were hung up to be cooked, and the screaming wounded bodies. When they reached the spot where the women and children had emerged they poured walls of flame down into the underground tunnel system for a long time. Then they started forward again, unstoppable, like messengers from hell, bringing a little sample of it with them. They set every square inch of what had once been the bandit encampment aflame until it looked like the burning surface of Jupiter.

Stone stumbled onto the side of the tank, then up a half-dozen hidden footholds. He came down inside the ladder and stared hard at Lieutenant Carpenter, who was looking quite pleased, as were the rest of the Bradley's crew.

"What was that all about?" Stone asked. "Those people were under a white flag. More than that, they were women and children."

"Colonel," the lieutenant exclaimed, looking at Stone with surprise. "We *never* take prisoners on a search-and-destroy mission. Those orders come from the very top—from General Patton. It's always been that way. Those things down there weren't even human. Why, did you see how they looked?"

"Get out!" Stone suddenly said through clenched teeth.

"What?" Lieutenant Carpenter asked nervously, his contemptuous grin suddenly vanishing, not sure what Stone had said.

"I said, get out, all of you." He glared around the inside of the tank as if he were ready to kill every one of them. They all rose and slowly climbed the ladder and then out the top, looking back at the commander of the strike force as if he were absolutely insane. Stone pulled the hatch cover down hard and locked it from the inside. Then he sat down on the steel floor, put his head between his hands and cried like a baby.

CHAPTER
Seventeen

"A TOAST, Colonel Stone, I insist," General Patton exclaimed, his face just inches from Stone's, his hand holding a crystal snifter filled with the finest brandy, which swirled like liquid fire inside.

"General, I—I—," Stone started, then stopped again, not having the slightest idea of how to explain his feelings. If the man didn't know it was wrong to kill women and children, it was not exactly something he would be able to convince him of. Stone knew he had to go very slowly and carefully here. He had just sort of let events carry him along up until now, like a leaf on a river. But now Stone had to figure this whole thing out, and fast.

"Relax, Colonel, relax," Patton said, letting his hand rest on Stone's shoulder. "Here, again I insist. Humor an old general. It is a ritual that I carry out after all my victorious battles with those officers who helped bring them to successful fruition. And you, Stone, have carried out an eminently successful engagement—with the least number of casualties, I might add, that we've taken on any large search-and-destroy for nearly a year. It's just as I hoped; you're high-level material, Stone. You've shown up at the right time, I'll damned well tell you that!" The general laughed again, standing up. His eyes were so filled with seeing his ambitions for so many years so close to completion that he didn't see the pain in Stone's eyes—the strange look that he now wore, like that of a haunted man.

And Stone was haunted. Haunted by the faces of those sobbing women, the snot-nosed kids hanging onto their mothers' tattered clothes. Haunted by the blood mist that had filled the air for long minutes after they were all banished from the face of this earth with merciless sheets of hellfire. Haunted even though he had ordered his troops to halt, even though he had cried. But tears weren't enough to overcome blood. Martin Stone was now a possessed man, the faces of those innocent dead hovering around him like vultures made of the darkest material.

"Drink! Drink!" Patton said, putting one of the pear-shaped crystal snifters into Stone's hand and pushing up. Stone let the hand be guided. He felt dazed, confused, unsure in a way that he had never felt before. He lifted the blue crystal glass to his lips and gulped it down, hoping it would erase the image of a white flag whipping in the air from his mind. But it didn't.

"General," Stone suddenly spoke loudly as he let the drained glass fall to his side. "General, there were women and children out there. They were under a white flag. I commanded the men to stop, but they fired—wiped them out. They told me this was under your direct standing order."

"Of course, of course it was my direct order, Stone," Patton said impatiently, filling his brandy glass again, this time to the top. He sipped it, walked around his office and then addressed Stone from across the luxurious room. "Look, Colonel Stone, we must eradicate a disease. Stop it before it starts. If allowed to live, those women, those children would just create more of their own. You saw what they were like —flesh eaters. These cannot be allowed to live. Stone, it is nothing but pure logic. America must be cleansed, purified, before she has the slightest chance to be resurrected. This we do, Stone. As we conquer we purify. As we slowly retake the wastelands, we cleanse them all. We are like a flame, a burning flame that destroys and fertilizes at the same time."

Stone reached his hand out for a refill. He needed it. The general poured the snifter full and Stone pulled the glass back to his mouth and drained it fast.

"Tell me, General, I know it's a little far off . . . but just what kind of world do you visualize creating when you've conquered everyone out there? When there's no more fighting to do."

"Oh, that's a hell of a long way down the pike." Patton laughed. "But it's a legitimate question, and I won't lie and say I've never thought about it. Because I have. What great man wouldn't . . . in his most tranquil moments. I visualize a world of order, Stone. That is what man needs. Order and control. Humanity has misunderstood its own nature for much of man's history. All these . . . governments have been tried—democracy, parliamentary . . . But you know what, Stone. The truth is, people want to be ruled. They desire to be told what to do, led like sheep through gates. Told what to think, dream, eat and shit. Humankind are most happy when they're most controlled. Like the army, Stone. That's why men want to join me, want to become a part of this growing military empire. Because they want order. They want to be told to jump . . . and heel . . . and kill. So I *will* create such a world, Stone. A world where people will finally get what they actually want. A system of law and order that will last a thousand years, ten thousand years. A society in which there will be no crime, no dissension. The first truly perfect society in history."

"I see," Stone said softly, starting for the first time to get the full picture of what he had gotten himself into. "I see."

"And that is exactly why the human gene pool must be purified," the general went on, his eyes fiery. "If it is all allowed to just keep blending and reproducing together, there will never be peace; there will always be these disruptive elements. Thus, the misfits, the social lowlifes, the flesh eaters, the negroid race and all the other troublemakers must all be removed. When the race is pure and white the way it was when the country began, then there will be order, and true equality among men who are equals."

"I see," Stone muttered dumbly again, as Patton's bloody plans came into further focus. And suddenly Martin Stone knew one thing above all else: he had to stop this man. Patton was far more of a danger than those he was wiping out, a million times more dangerous. They were isolated, savage, with no more interest in taking over the whole damned country than in colonizing the moon. They just wanted their own little piece of the mountain, the highway, and they would just kill and/or eat whomever came along. Even the Mafia, and the ruthless biker gangs of the Guardians of Hell were all too shortsighted and too greedy to see beyond their own little provinces, their own immediate desire. Only Patton, of all the dark minds he had met, had plans to take it all—the whole damned pie of America— and leave a river of blood behind, composed of half the races in the country, to do it. And then a nice fascist Third

Reich type arrangement to last "a thousand years." Patton
was far more dangerous than any of those he killed, because
he had a chance to succeed. A damned good chance at that.

On the spur of the moment Stone made up his mind. April
was going to have to wait a little longer. Stone had to figure
out a way—impossible as it seemed—to stop the military
juggernaut that the NAA was rapidly becoming. Nothing
was more important. Stone knew he was going to have to
play a con game par excellence if he was going to pull this
whole thing off. He plastered a smile on his face, grateful
for all the recent practice, and looked up at Patton, who was
standing in front of the Michelangelo he had promised
Stone, with an almost lewd grin on his face.

"Don't you wish to collect your reward, Colonel Stone?"
Patton asked from across the room.

"Ah yes, my painting," Stone said, rising and walking
over to the wall-to-wall masterpiece. He ran his fingers just
over the surface of the painting as if stroking an expensive
silk. Patton appreciated the gesture of possession, that the
art mattered to Stone not because of its beauty but because
he owned it. Because through the giving of wealth and pro-
motions, Patton knew he could control the young man he
was already beginning to dimly picture as being a possible
successor to himself. A hardly conceived notion, one he
wouldn't readily admit even to himself, but someday far in
the future, perhaps . . .

"Yes, I was thinking about this magnificent painting when
I was out there in the battlefield," Stone said. "You're right.
Beauty does give one a strong motivation to succeed. And
my dog—and bike—as we agreed."

"Of course, of course," Patton said, waving at him and
wincing in mock disgust. "That's already old hat, Stone. I
still don't think you totally understand. Whatever's out there

is ours, yours, mine. The wealth of an entire civilization is ours for the picking. We're like . . . gods now." Stone noticed his inclusion in the word "gods." So Patton had allowed him to such illustrious heights. The general poured another load into Stone's glass, and then his own. They were both starting to get a little drunk.

"Go ahead," Patton said, pointing at the Michelangelo. "Take it."

"You mean just rip it right out of the frame and roll it up, just like that?" Stone asked a little incredulously.

"That's exactly what I mean, Colonel. We made an agreement—I always pay off." Stone took out his blade and pried the outer part of the gold gilded frame that held the masterpiece in place. He carefully pulled the immense painting from the wall, put it on the floor and rolled the whole thing up like a rug to be taken to the cleaners.

Patton looked at him slyly. "So you're no longer concerned with the no prisoner policy? I wouldn't, after all, ask any man to do something his conscience wouldn't allow," Patton said, which Stone figured to be the biggest lie of the night.

"No," the younger man said, forcing a smile. "After hearing your full description of your plans for total conquest, I understand it all better. And I must say I couldn't agree with you more. I thought this massacre had been an indication of cruelty by the NAA. But that's not the case at all. It's a policy, not an emotion. You don't kill out of hatred, but scientifically, in a controlled manner, to further a goal of complete order, complete law in the future."

"Exactly, exactly," General Patton said excitedly. He had rarely heard it so well put. "You almost read my mind, Stone," he said with a laugh. "We kill in a scientific manner to insure complete law in the future." He mouthed the words

Stone had just spoken, and liked how they sounded. "I should have you write my speeches, Stone. Going to need some soon . . . when we start entering the next stage in reconquest."

"Glad to be of any service I can to the Third Army," Stone said. General Patton poured him yet another drink, looking close into his eyes through his own slightly hazed-over half drunken orbs. He stared hard at Stone, as if trying to comprehend if the man was entirely trustworthy, if all was as it seemed. But he wanted to believe too much, too hard. And so he looked deep into the lying eyes of Martin Stone . . . and believed his every word.

CHAPTER
Eighteen

"STONE, WE'RE going for a ride," Patton suddenly said, grabbing a fur-collared trenchcoat from a rack. "I'm bringing you in on this operation all the way. All the way." Stone finished his drink with one big gulp. Jesus, it seemed like every second took him deeper into this thing; he was booked for the ride now, that was for damned sure—all the way to the end. He looked over at the general, who had already strapped on his ivory-handled .45's—he never went out without them on. "Come on, Colonel Stone, America awaits us. Let us not delay a nation's destiny to be reborn out of fire."

"Indeed," Stone answered, putting down the empty glass. He picked up the rolled up Michelangelo on the floor, threw it over his shoulder and headed toward the door. He was glad he had had the shots of brandy. It would make it a little easier for him to go through this whole charade. The general strode like a Caesar with omnipotent pride and rigid determination down the hall to his private garage at the back of his headquarters. Elite troops, all wearing the gold eagle, guarded every doorway, every entrance and exit. They stood even taller, stiffer than the general himself, if that were possible, and snapped out stiff-fisted salutes as he stalked past, Stone fast on his heels. Patton went through a metal door and into a garage filled with vehicles—jeeps, motorcycles, even a tank, just in case. He led Stone to a thickly armored half-track with huge solid rubber tires, high up on double-reinforced frame. The thing looked invulnerable. Patton jumped up one side, Stone the other and the general quickly started the armored vehicle.

"If there's trouble, Stone," he said with a little grin, almost as if he wished there would be, "the machine-gun controls are there." He pointed toward the center of the vehicle, where a machine gun sat welded inside a little mobile tower from which the firer could spray the weapon a full three-sixty degrees. Patton eased the thing into gear and started slowly forward. Two guards pulled open high steel gates that moved on a pulley system and they spread smoothly apart. The half-track headed out the doors and down a ramp into the dark night. The general had driven only about a hundred feet up to one of several back entrances to Fort Bradley before the guards on patrol at a machine-gun post saw the supreme commander flag snapping in the air on the front of the vehicle, and ran double time to open the gate.

Within minutes they were hauling ass down a fairly solid paved road heading into the darkest part of night. The general had even flipped on the half shielded headlights of the half-track so he could see and make better time, though it was actually NAA official policy to run blind at night outside of the fort. But then, he had dictated that policy. So he could dispense with it as well. He was feeling reckless to-

night. It was all coming together faster than he had hoped.
Faster than he had dreamed.

"Are you ready?" he suddenly asked Stone, who was staring up into the few sprinkles of stars that peered down
through the overcast sky. But all he kept seeing was the
faces of those women, those kids, some of them had been
fucking babies sucking at their mothers' breasts. The faces
of those burning dead, blazing in place of the stars, took up
the sky wherever he looked.

"I said, are you ready?" Patton repeated louder to Stone,
as he stepped harder on the gas pedal. "Ready to hear the
next step, the next stage on our road to total victory?"

"Yes, General," Stone said, turning and trying to focus his
eyes on the man. "And anxious to know every detail."

"There's a meeting going to happen, Stone, a meeting of
nearly all the Mafia, biker gangs and warlords for the whole
Rocky Mountain and Plains area. A meeting scheduled for
two days from now. They have one every year to work out
inter-gang problems, pay each other off—take care of their
slimy business. If we could take out that entire crew at one
stroke, we could take control of an immense area of land—
nearly seven states in a matter of weeks, rather than the
years it would take with town-by-town fighting between our
forces and each little chapter of the bastards out there. No,
I'm going to take them all at once, Stone, grab them up in
my hands." He gripped the wheel of the half-track with
white-knuckled fists. "And squeeze them until the flesh on
their bodies turns to pulp, until they melt before me."

"Sounds like a great idea," Stone said, sitting up straight
in the leather seat of the half-track, trying to sound as enthusiastic about the flesh-squeezing idea as possible. "Huh . . .
just how are you going to attack, sir?" Stone asked a little
hesitantly, not sure how the general would take to his pet

project being questioned. "I've seen some of their forces; they're pretty well armed. I would imagine at a convention of that size they would be extremely well protected. I wonder if your Third Army is ready to take on an army nearly as large as itself at this stage in time."

"Precisely," Patton said, glancing at Stone, his eyes burning like blue laser rubies again. "My realization exactly. Except for one thing, Stone, my ace in the hole. My way to melt the sons-of-bitches down to ash without losing a single one of my own."

"You keep saying melt, General," Stone said curiously. "What do you have in mind—setting the convention site on fire?"

"On fire." Patton laughed. "Yes, you might say that. A fire that will cleanse with utter purity, will leave a clean slate upon which to build." He squinted at the weaving road ahead as they hit a sudden deep crack and bounced over it, flying through the air on one side for a second or two and then landing with a thud. "You'll see soon enough, Stone. See what our ace in the hole is."

He drove for about an hour and Stone vaguely kept track of where they were going, mentally noting a particular rock formation off to the side, or a group of trees configured a certain way on the semi-mountainous terrain around them. Suddenly they were there—wherever there was—and Patton slowed as he came to what Stone could only make out as a patch of darkness. Lights snapped on in front of them and gruff voices yelled out challenges as Stone heard the safetys of at least two machine guns being switched off. Then whoever was in the darkness saw the general and a flurry of feet came from behind the searchlights as a gate was opened. As they drove on Stone could see they were inside a protected area approximately a hundred feet in diameter and dead

ahead of them was a large cone-shaped piece of steel built
on top of a concrete square. The shape and design looked
strangely familiar. Suddenly his heart skipped a beat. It was
a silo. A missile silo.

"Come on, Colonel Stone," the general said, leading him
out of the half-track to what looked like a piece of flat
ground next to the silo. But Patton reached down, gripped a
hidden handle and pulled a steel door up. He started down
inside and Stone followed just behind, resting his feet and
hands on a wide rung ladder. He looked down and felt a
wave of dizziness sweep over him. They were inside the
silo—on a ladder that went straight down what looked like
hundreds of feet. And taking up the center of the ten-foot-
wide, perfectly round funnel was the biggest goddamned
missile Stone had ever seen, poised, ready to fly up into the
blackest of nights.

"Isn't it beautiful," Patton screamed up to Stone. "I mean,
isn't it just about the most beautiful goddamned thing you've
ever seen, Colonel Stone?"

"Absolutely," Stone yelled down, examining the missile
closely as he moved down the narrow ladder that ran right
alongside it. The thing was thick, a lot wider somehow than
he had imagined a missile to be—and long too. It seemed to
go on forever as they moved down the ladder. It was a metallic blue, and seamless, perfect every inch that Stone
looked. There was a feeling about it. God, was there a feeling about it. Just being next to it—though the weapon was
absolutely still and silent—he could feel its tremendous
power to destroy, to kill. A shiver ran up and down his spine
and he had the strongest urge to get away from the steel
rocket, just get away, run as fast as he could. But he held
himself in place and kept descending deeper into the bowels
of the silo.

"Jesus, she's a sight, isn't she," Patton asked Stone as he dropped to a circular walkway at the very base of the silo. "This particular design of missile, the M-7, has always been my favorite, Colonel. The lines, the thick wide body, the immense double-stage rocket with nearly enough power to send this thing into orbit. I mean, it's almost more like a Russian rocket, only this one's got the computerized guidance and avoidance systems that the Russkies never could get together."

"You're quite a connoisseur of missiles, I see," Stone commented dryly as he looked up the inside of the silo. The damned thing looked bigger, if anything, from below. It made him feel small, about as vulnerable as an ant with a combat boot hanging just over its head.

"Yes, as a matter of fact, in my earlier days, before the shit hit the societal fan, I was attached to a missile base, in charge of its security and military operations. I learned all about missiles then. Everything about them, from their maintenance to their firing." He led Stone around the walkway, reaching out with his hand to touch the missile with his palm. He stroked it like the thigh of a woman, slowly, feeling every sensation, every nuance of the perfect curve of the metal.

"Tell me, Stone, how big do you think she is?"

"I couldn't hazard a guess," Stone answered, gulping, not really wanting to know.

"Oh come on, again humor an old man. What do you think?"

"Oh God," Stone muttered, feeling as if he were in a guess-how-many-jellybeans-are-in-the-jar-win-a-sundae contest. "Two megaton, five megaton . . . I don't know," Stone said. "I haven't been around too many H-bombs lately."

"Ten, Stone, ten megatons. And plutonium-enriched, one of the advanced models with equivalent power of the old fifteen meg or better."

"Can you actually make it . . . go?" Stone asked, feeling his chest growing tighter by the second, his lips and mouth drying out so they felt like a salt flat on a summer day.

"Go?" Patton laughed. "Colonel, I can pinpoint this missile to within one hundred yards in a 15,000 mile radius. You think this is all for show." He knocked on a two-inch-thick reinforced steel door and a face peered through the leaded Plexiglas window. Then it opened and they walked in. Again Stone was overwhelmed and fought not to have any of it register on his face—the sheer insane power these men possessed. The room was filled with radar screens and computer printouts, constantly updating weather, oil pressure on hydraulics systems, electrical hookups—every goddamned thing it took to keep an atomic missile alive, and to be able to send its flaming ass into the clouds.

"This is Colonel Stone," the general said, introducing him to the two technicians who sat on duty, far apart on each end of the nearly eighty-foot-long control center. "And these are Major Rasner and Major Hollings, in charge of the actual launch operations. We're set up here just like the old days. It takes both men to turn keys simultaneously to arm the missile and send her up. Both men are chained to their seats, so if one goes mad we have a safety. And as you can see—" He swept his hands around the blinking beeping high tech missile control room that made Stone feel more like he was in a spaceship headed for the outer planets than a concrete-reinforced bunker two hundred feet below the desert soil.

"And who decides when and where to actually launch the missile," Stone asked as he tried to see where the launch controls were. "Assuming," he coughed, "that one were ever pushed to such an eventuality."

"Oh, one doesn't have to be pushed, Colonel Stone." The general's laugh was a thin rasp. His tone and volume suddenly dropped lower and he stared at Stone as a madman might stare into the void. "I have already decided to use the weapon. In three days, in fact. And it's targeted for Glenwood Springs, where the warlords of crime and blood are having their annual who-gets-how-much-of-what's-left-of-America meeting. Only, you know what's ironic, Colonel Stone?" the general asked. "There won't be enough left of them to divvy anything up. Instead there will be a tremendous power vacuum created throughout the central United States, and the NAA will move in—seize the opening and take control in a blitzkrieg of armored vehicles and highly mobile, combat-hardened soldiers."

"You're—go—ing to use this bomb?" Stone asked, knowing the target was less than a hundred miles away. The man was mad. He'd take himself out too. He'd take the whole damned state and—perhaps, if the winds were right —a few others with it.

"Goddamned right, I'm going to use this bomb," Patton half shouted, whirling at Stone. His eyes suddenly looked wild, a storm swirling behind the ice blue.

"Sir, I hate to be negative," Stone said hesitantly, "but I do feel it's important for an officer, such as myself, to question certain things, just play devil's advocate for a moment. You yourself said everyone around you were all fools and yes men. That you needed me just for that quality of questioning. Of adding another perspective."

"Yes, yes, go ahead," Patton said impatiently, folding his arms and looking up at the waveform monitor on the far wall—waving lines of luminescent green that wriggled in digital data concerning the electronic health of the missile across a wide tilted screen.

"Sir." Stone coughed, trying to remember his debating class rules back at college—what the hell were they? Establish need, find flaw, give alternative and correct approach. Find flaw—he sure as hell could do that. "Sir," Stone said, looking over at Patton, who wouldn't return his glance but kept staring at the slithering sine waves, his chin and profile posed sideways in a most heroic stance. The man knew how to look like a general, Stone thought. You had to give him that.

"Sir, as I remember my A-bombs—and grant you I'm not the authority that you are—the amount of radiation released from a ten megaton H-bomb only a hundred miles away would have a very powerful effect on all of us here at Fort Bradley, in fact all over Colorado. I mean it's not just the blast, but the fallout, the radioactivity in the wind, in the grass, in the—"

"Oh, don't give me all that liberal ecology bullshit," Patton said, his jaw tightening even farther, as if he could keep the truth out by clenching his cheekbones a little harder. "I'm surprised at you, Colonel Stone, quite surprised."

"Well, sir, it's not that I don't think the scum should be blasted into infinity, but if we nuke them we're guaranteed to hit ourselves. It's a proven fact. Why right here ... somewhere ... there must be a booklet, a chart or something, showing the damage done at different ranges. Is there?" Stone asked, going over to one of the technicians, who opened a drawer without saying a word and handed Stone a thick manual that looked like an *Everything You Always Wanted to Know About the H-Bomb But You Were Afraid It Would Kill You* kind of text. It was about six inches thick, hard to hold with one hand.

"Page 1,879," the tech said with a bored tone. Stone leafed to the page and found it. "There, sir," he said, handing the bible-sized manual to the general, who took it gruffly and then, glaring around angrily at them all, took out a pair of reading glasses from the inside of his coat and looked at the picture—a map with concentric circles leading outwards, showing the damage from a ten megaton missile at ten-mile intervals. At one hundred miles the damage was, to say the least, severe. A windblown storm of radioactive debris would sweep through the area, not to mention the fallout that would occur over the next few days. Estimated: fifty percent fatalities within six months—human and animal. Water supply contaminated; food chain, livestock, fish and crops dangerously contaminated. In short, a mess. As Chernobyl in the Soviet Union had proved years before, a little went a long way when it came to radiation damage—and a plutonium-enriched ten meg went a long, long way.

"Sir," Stone said, trying to strike while the iron was hot, "perhaps the fact is that it's not so important to destroy the crime bosses as to remove them from their stations of power. We could use the sheer destructive potential of the weapon as a negotiating point. They surrender to us, or we send them into Hell. Diplomacy, I have always thought," Stone said slyly, "was the hallmark of great leadership. I think you have an opportunity here to not fire a shot, and win everything. The military history books would look favorably upon such an accomplishment."

"Yes, I see your point," the general said, brightening slightly as he began to see the possibilities of such a move. "But how . . . who—"

"General," Stone said, stepping a little closer to Patton and talking softer, trying to lure him into the concept as one tried to dance a fly in front of a mountain trout, "if we could give them some kind of proof—the cover of this manual, *Maintenance and Firing of the M-7*—for example, and convince them they didn't have a chance. Maybe even bring four or five of their top leaders—under blindfold, of course —to the silo and show them with their own eyes. It is the use of power, General, not the sheer dispensing of it, that marks the great strategist," Stone said with sincerity, remembering the phrase that had always been a favorite of his father's.

"I admit, it's an interesting concept—purely theoretically, of course. But somehow I imagine the carrying out of it would be almost impossible. How would this threat be conveyed? Why would their people even trust us enough to come? They would certainly kill me if they had me in their grasp—you can rest assured of that." He had taken the bait; Stone moved in for the hooking.

"*I'll* go, sir. As you can see, I'm very persuasive. Why, I've even got you interested. Plus, some of those sons-of-bitches know me. I've had my own run-ins with them several times. They hate me, but they know I'm not a liar. I think I could get them to at least listen. What harm would it do?"

"You'd risk your life, Colonel Stone?" Patton asked skeptically. "You could end up with your hands and feet missing and your balls sewn into your mouth. They've done it to some of my intelligence men who were trying to infiltrate their ranks."

"Well, I'm willing to take the chance, General. They're my hands, my feet, my everything."

"Why, Stone, why?" Patton asked, suddenly looking very suspicious as if he smelled a trap, as if Stone was in with the bastards.

"Sir, you said you liked knowing men's motivations so

you could keep a hold over them. Well, mine is greed. I'm not ashamed to admit it. I want more. I want—as you yourself put it—everything. If I carry out this mission, General, I want a mansion, enough expensive art and beautiful women to fill it, enough money to keep it going the rest of my life . . . and enough weapons to guard it so no son-of-a-bitch can take it away from me. I'll risk my life—for everything. Bet it all on a single toss of the dice. That's why I'm willing to take the chance, General, for greed."

"Greed is the American way, Stone," Patton replied, his eyes half closed as if he were looking at Stone from out of a pillbox gun slit. "All right, Colonel, you're on. I've always been a gambling man. Your balls against a life of ultra-wealth. But if you don't come back, I'm sending up the M-7, and let the chips fall where they may."

CHAPTER
Nineteen

WITHIN TWELVE hours a convoy of NAA vehicles tore across the canyon wastelands toward Glenwood Springs—four armored jeeps with 105mm recoilless rifles in the lead, followed by three tanks. Mountain bandits eyed the force with curious eyes from their hiding places amongst the boulders and the scraggly pine-covered hills. But none of them dared attack, not against that. With rifles, pistols, a grenade or two, they wouldn't have a chance. Stone sat in the lead tank, at the controls. He felt confident enough now to drive one on his own. Besides, if the dim plans that were beginning to formulate in his mind as to just how he was going to sort this whole thing out came to pass, he'd better know how to use one of these. He'd need it. The driver of the Bradley III sat in a metal swivel chair a yard away, looking pissed as hell but unable to say a word since Stone was in charge of the entire mission.

He'd gotten Patton to give him two days—one to get

there, and one to convince the crime bosses that they'd better give it up or their asses were grass, smoking atomic
grass. Then he would transmit the results on a small battery-
powered transmitter that he carried with him. No signal—in
exactly forty-eight hours—would mean they had cut him
up, and the missile would be launched, no ifs, ands or buts.

Stone knew there were spies and assassins throughout the
crew. Patton would trust Stone on such a mission only as far
as a bullet could strike his flesh. Stone felt the pressure. He
had never been in a tighter spot in his life and beads of sweat
kept lining up along his forehead and dripping down his
face. He tried to keep his mind on the driving of the tank.
He liked the handling of the battle machine; it moved fast,
quick to the touch, almost like a good sports car. It was
amazing that such a heavy machine could move with such
on-a-dime maneuverability. Still, it was hard not to notice all
the eyes peering at him from the rest of the tank's crew, or to
forget the terms of the wager—his balls against . . . No, no,
he didn't want to think about it. Didn't want to get a mental
picture of that knife coming down and—

"Sir, as long as we're driving all night," the captain of the
tank, Captain Chambers, spoke up, realizing that since
Stone might well soon be one of the most important men in
the NAA it might be a good idea to get on his good side.
"Perhaps I could demonstrate some of the other features of
the Bradley. It can actually do quite a lot, you know."

Stone was glad to be pulled from his dark musings. "Yes,
show me everything, Captain. That would be an excellent
idea." And so through the moonless night, driving the tank
on infrared video, Stone absorbed everything he could about
the Bradley—its computer and radar systems, its ground-to-
ground missiles, capable of taking out the side of a building,

and all the other extras that made a tank like the Bradley III such a handy thing to drive.

They made excellent time across the backlands, which for all their desolation and terrible fissured beauty were fairly open and flat. The convoy roared forward through the night, a tail of dust rising high above them that lasted for miles. By the time morning was just beginning to break in a gray waterfall of light from the east, they were there. The force stopped on a plateau overlooking the town of Glenwood Springs about three miles away. Stone climbed the ladder up to the top of the tank and stepped out, taking out his field glasses. He crouched down so as not to make a silhouette against the silver sky and peered through the binoc's.

There was something going on down there, that was for damned sure. There were cars, bizarrely armored vehicles everywhere along the streets. Garbage was strewn wildly about and Stone thought he could see some bodies here and there amidst the general filth of the place. They were not just meeting, but having their fun too, as they always did. Whenever Stone had been around these bastards before, there had always been a waste heap of bodies left behind in their wake.

He gathered the other officers and went over their plans. Stone would go below with one tank; the others would stay here on the hill and get their cannons targeted on the town. If he wasn't back within twenty-four hours, they were to open fire and then get the hell out of there as fast as possible. Stone didn't explain the second part. They'd find out soon enough. The crew of his tank were all volunteers—including Colonel Garwood—one of the brass that Stone liked and trusted the least. They all knew the risks going down there, but like Stone they also knew the rewards they would accrue for the successful completion of such a risky operation. Some men will do anything for wealth, or country.

The guards at the north end of the town—a gang of bikers with their motorcycles parked in a row, blocking movement —stood up and stared with amazement at the tank that came grinding down the road toward them. They knew that more crime bosses were expected, but somehow hadn't expected any to show up in a tank. The Bradley stopped about ten yards away from the line of bikes and one of the bigger gang members, with black leather jacket and chains draped over his arms like an admiral, walked up to the barricade of motorcycles as Stone emerged from the top of the tank.

"Name?" the biker yelled out, pulling out his checklist to look for the entry.

"Name's Stone, Colonel Stone," he yelled back from the tank. "But I'm not on the party list so don't bother looking for me!"

"Then what the hell do you want, mister? This ain't exactly the neck of the woods to be fucking around in."

"I want to talk to the top bosses," Stone said coolly. "I've got an offer they can't refuse."

"Sorry, mister," the biker said, waving his hand for Stone to just drive off. "I mean, your tank looks impressive and all, but I got orders not to let no one in who ain't on the list. So before I send a radio signal for the artillery unit located up there on that building . . ." He pointed to a church steeple in the center of town from which a steel barrel projected, gleaming in the morning sun, which was just rising over the Rockies.

"Oh, so that's where it is," Stone yelled above the whine of the tank's idling engine. He leaned into the hatch of the tank and yelled down. "Sight up the top of that church steeple and let her have it." The entire turret on which he was sitting began turning and the 120mm cannon quickly raised up like the head of a cobra.

"What the hell are you—" the biker yelled back, his face growing white. But the words were cut off as the Bradley shook back on its treads and the cannon roared with a ten-foot-long burp of fire. The bikers could hear the shell screaming overhead; that is, for the one second before it hit. Then the entire top of the church—used in the last five years for far different purposes than what it had been intended—exploded in a whirlwind of wood and flesh and red spray that spewed out over the whole center of the town. When the immediate storm of dust settled slightly they could see there was nothing left above the second floor. Nothing.

"Take her forward," Stone yelled down through the hatch and the Bradley instantly lurched forward. The biker jumped back in horror as the others, who had been leaning against their motorcycles in a bored manner, were suddenly wide awake and clearing a way. There's not many men who will stand up to the steel face of a tank bearing straight down on them. The Bradley rode right up on four of the bikes, knocking them down and half crushing them beneath it as the treads ground over the vehicles, twisting and crushing them like some kind of mobile car-flattening machine. He ordered the tank to stop just the other side of the barricade in a large square.

"Need more demonstrations before you go tell them?" Stone asked with a satisfied smile, looking down at about a dozen of the black-jacketed gang, who were cowering back against a brick wall.

"No—I—I'll go," the biker leader stuttered. He ran side-ways in front of the tank, keeping his bulging eyes on the huge cannon pointing straight at his head. The others fol-

lowed suit, like scampering chickens after their mother hen.
Stone had definitely made an impression.

Within minutes he was being led into the main meeting
hall of the crime bosses—an old skating rink with an arching domed plastic ceiling that let in streams of filtered light
from above. The assembled bosses sat on wooden seats all
around the perimeter of where the ice floor had been—now
plywood sheets nailed down to make a floor over the rusted
gridded piping of ice-making equipment. The general had
been right about one thing, Stone saw the moment he walked
into the large open space, there were a hell of a lot of the
bastards here. His eyes quickly scanned the rows of seats
stretching all the way around the place, filled almost to capacity. There were a good thousand of them, from Mafia
capos in their double-breasted suits to Guardian of Hell
chieftains with golden chains on their shoulders marking
their rank; from wild-eyed bandits with belts of grenades
crisscrossed around their chests to subhuman mountain men
dressed in badly sewn bearskin hides. They were all there.
The whole rotten crew had turned out for this one.

"And what, may I ask," a voice spoke loudly above the
murmur of voices throughout the ex-rink, "may we do for
you before we kill you." Stone saw the source of the words
—a man sitting with three other hard-looking fellows behind
what looked like some sort of makeshift judge's bench. They
all wore long black robes and were staring down at him with
most unpleasant expressions, as were all one thousand of the
toughest, meanest and most psychotic looking dudes Martin
Stone had ever seen. Colonel Garwood stood behind Stone,
almost shaking in his boots. Stone glared at the man for a
split second to cool him out. To show fear in front of these
bastards was tantamount to committing suicide. That's why
Stone had taken out the church—he knew they respected

power above all else, firepower especially. And right now he had the biggest gun in town.

"I'll get right to the point," Stone said, turning slightly as he spoke so most of them could hear him. He wanted them all to get the message, to truly understand just what was at stake here. "There's an atomic missile targeted on this very building right at this instant. By merely touching a dial on this radio transmitter," Stone lied, as it would take a lot more than that to get it going, "I can signal for it to be launched. And if you started running the second I pressed the button, you know what?" Stone asked again, looking around at them as two thousand pairs of eyes glared back like glowing knives. "As far as you could run, drive or even fly, it would get you. It would get you and melt you right down to your bones like plastic melting on a toy soldier, and then even your bones would smoke and melt too. And that's the God's honest truth."

"Who the fuck is this guy?" another voice yelled from the crowd.

"Kill him! Shoot the asshole now!" another scarred face suggested, rising and pulling out a .45 that looked heavily used.

"Hold it!" the judge or whatever he was screamed above the din and stood up from his chair with a 30–30 Winchester, holding it high across his chest. "Shut up, you assholes, and sit down!" the head judge commanded them—and with shoulders as wide as a table and a sallow and almost concave face that bore not a little resemblance to Boris Karloff, even the toughest of the tough were persuaded to head back down into their seats and put their firepower down.

"Go on, Colonel Stone," the black-robed crime judge said more quietly as he sat again but kept the rifle in plain view.

Apparently the gathered criminal elements had their own etiquette when it came to keeping order. "Tell me more."

"I've been sent under order of General Patton of the Third Army. He has instructed me to tell you that he demands your unconditional surrender within twenty-four hours, or you and everyone within fifty miles of here is radioactive ashes."

Again there were numerous disturbances around the arena, and before Stone knew what was happening the judge stood up quickly in his seat and gripped the rifle to his cheek. He pulled the trigger and snapped down the lever, firing again and again in a blur of motion. Some bearded, wolf-hide-covered thug with pistol in his hand went flying from his chair and tumbled onto the plywood floor of the rink. He twitched a few times, riddled with slugs in an almost perfect straight line from nose to navel, as a pool of blood bubbled into a little brook beneath him.

This time the congregation grew very still and again the judge urged Stone to go on.

"That's the story," Stone said, now addressing just the judges since it was obvious—that at least inside here—they ran the show. "I'm to radio back your reply, and then either take you prisoner . . . or see us all die in hellfire."

"How do we know you're telling the truth?" the head judge asked. Stone started walking slowly toward the raised judges' platform about eighty feet away, but five men appeared out of nowhere, each holding an Ingram submachine gun, and stopped him short.

"No one may approach the judges' bench," one of the men said, his face like something that had been left in the blender too long.

"Then give him this," Stone said, pulling open the cover of the missile manual and the chart showing damage at different ranges from his jacket. He handed it to the man and stepped back next to Colonel Garwood, who looked as if he were about to shit in his pants under the burning gaze of the rabble. The face-mashed guard took them over to the judges' bench and the four black-robed men looked at the pages closely, passing them to one another. They conferred for several minutes, whispering back and forth. Then the head judge spoke up again.

"It is possible, from this evidence, that what you say is true—possible but not conclusive."

"Judge, your honor, whatever your proper title is, it's all true, I swear to you, every word I've told you. But though I *was* sent here to attempt to get you to surrender, the fact is I'm going to help you, show you a way out. I'm going to lead you right back to their camp, and help you destroy Patton and the Third Army." Colonel Garwood stared at Stone with his jaw literally hanging open as he heard the traitorous words.

"Why should you do this, Stone?" the head judge asked through his cadaverous-looking white lips. "Help us when all we want to do is kill you."

"Because I've seen what General Patton really intends for America—a Brave New World of genetically selected sheep ruled by laws and regulations that make Hitler look like a boy scout leader. I was in his inner circle and I know what he has in mind. Don't get me wrong, your honor, I hate your kind. I've spent the last few months of my life fighting scum like you—killing a lot of them too. But I know, just because you bastards are such savages, so greedy in your provincial little ways, that you will always be divided, will always be squabbling to protect your own little fiefdoms. You will never be the threat that he is. And for this one moment, you and I are on the same side. Then we can go about our business of trying to destroy one another. Because make no mistake about it, I hate you, and the anarchy and blood for which you stand. But right now I hate Patton more, because he *could* do it. He *could* send America into the Dark Ages that will last ten thousand years."

"You fucking traitor," Colonel Garwood suddenly screamed as he stood alongside him, listening to Stone's little speech, his face growing redder and redder. "I always knew you weren't to be trusted from the very start. They should have let you go over the falls, you goddamned Benedict Arnold." He went for his .45 and had it halfway out when about twenty firearms went off simultaneously. The punctured body did a hideous little shuffle across the floor as if skating on its own blood and then slammed face first into the plywood, dead before its nose crushed into bloody putty on the wood.

Stone stood absolutely still, his hands raised so they didn't think he was going for anything. But the guns disappeared again and just the smoke and the scent of blood remained in the air.

"Colonel Stone," the head judge said, his face looking even more somber than before. "I think I believe you."

CHAPTER
Twenty

I T WAS perhaps the strangest army that had ever rumbled across the face of the earth: the tanks and jeeps of Stone's detachment—minus NAA troops who had been eliminated—in the lead, followed by the Mafia chieftains in their armored limousines, then hundreds of the Guardians of Hell atop their bikes, their battle colors flying, and behind them the countless smaller warlords from the mountains and plains in jeeps, old pickup trucks with swing machine guns mounted on the back, and every other damned thing on wheels that could still get up a head of steam and crank its way down a road. They drove into the descending night in a long stretched-out, ragged line, engines whining and screaming and pounding as a dim web of stars started to light up above, like Christmas lights not quite plugged in properly, through the sheer veil of a high cloud curtain.

Stone didn't feel at all good about the whole thing. His stomach felt like it was churning with bitter acids that were

ripping him apart. He had sent the radio signal telling Patton
that the crime bosses had surrendered and the general had
been overjoyed. And now? Now they would all think he was
a traitor. Not that it mattered. He did what he thought was
right. There were no two ways about it. You chose the side
you were on, and then you went all the way. He would take
the judgment when it came on his last day. But still, not all
of them were bad. If only Patton hadn't gone over the edge.
The general had been so close, so close to the right thing.
But he had gone off a cliff somewhere. The cliff of fascist
dreams. Why was it always like that? The son-of-a-bitch
was a genius, and in many ways a good man, yet he had lost
sight of the ball game and his own vainglorious schemes of
total conquest had taken over. It was the disease of powerful
and great men throughout history. Caesar, Alexander, Napoleon, Hitler, their very successes made them believe everything they did and thought was right. Therefore it should be
prescribed for the whole world. Then everything would be
better. Everyone would be happy under their totalitarian vision of life. It was simple. Right?

Wrong! Stone was in the way this time. All he could think
of was those women and kids turning into fire, screams frozen in the flames. Faces branded into his mind forever. And
there would be more—tens of thousands more, hundreds of
thousands perhaps. For with General Patton's purification-
by-fire mode of operation, as the Third Army swept across
the center of America they would liquidate all life not to
their immediate liking. Killing a man was one thing. Exter-
minating him was another.

No, Stone would take the heat. He was on the edge too.
The very edge, staring right into the fucking face of death.

"Colonel, Colonel!" Stone was startled from his dark
thoughts as he heard a voice talking to him. It was the head

judge, who was traveling with him in the lead tank. "Colonel Stone," the crime lord said, his white lips hardly moving as he spoke, "we'll be arriving at the outer limits of Fort Bradley's security perimeter within an hour if what you say is true. How exactly shall we proceed?" He was no longer wearing his black robe but a suit of something approaching leather armor from head to foot, and though bent over to fit into the cramped seating of the tank he still took up half the inside of the Bradley. The man was immense. Around his shoulder was an Ingram .45 machine pistol, and around his hips enough knives, pistols, grenades and other assorted implements of destruction to take on an army single-handed.

"We'll proceed exactly as planned," Stone said as he kept his eye on the video monitor of the road ahead. It showed him the infrared and radar readings interpreted digitally and reformatted into visual image—all in the space of a thousandth of a second. The thugs in the tank were all fascinated by the futuristic controls and kept staring around at everything with vastly entertained smiles on their faces. They'd all have some damned good drinking stories to share with their buddies back in whatever swamp or sewer they called home. There was nothing like killing. And high tech killing might be even more fun.

"We'll bring the force to coordinate B17-H28, as on this map here." Stone had the map displayed on a second screen to the left of his viewing terminal. "There you'll hold while I get inside and finish up a few things I have to do. Advance and firing on the fort shall commence at exactly six A.M., not one second later." Stone looked at the crime don, wondering if these dudes were going to really be able to use the tanks. He had given each of the judges about five hours of training. Not a hell of a lot. But these were the smartest of the lot, though that wasn't necessarily saying much by the looks of the crew that were following them. Still, they had been able to follow behind him in the other two tanks without crashing. Christ, the more he thought about this, the less chance it seemed they would succeed. But it was too late now. That was the understatement of the twentieth century.

"Better not be a trap, Stone," the judge said. "Or you're dead too."

"Not too many guys set a trap by bringing the enemy to the most strategically vulnerable point of his fortress and then tell them how to destroy him by using tank and artillery tactics formulated by Rommel and General Patton."

"Everything is twisted right now, Stone," the Mafia chief said, looking at Stone with those corpselike unmoving eyes, the skin stretched tight across his face as if it would crack and that flesh, so white, as pale as the flourescent face of the moon. "Who knows who to trust. You betray someone that we'll kill for you. But will you betray us? Will we kill you? Who is enemy and who friend?"

"There are no friends," Stone said bitterly as he started up the ladder and unsnapped the hatch above. "Only enemies who work together—and enemies who kill each other. Today we're on the same side. Tomorrow if I could I would probably try to kill you."

"And me the same," the don said with the first grudging little twist of his mouth indicating a smile. Somehow it was all humorous, a black joke beyond understanding. A joke played on the whole fucking human race.

"By the way, Stone, just for the record," the crime lord said, "your General Patton ain't no general. He's not even related to the World War II Patton. We've had our run-ins with the bastard before, and were able to dig up some records on him. He was a lousy captain when U.S. forces fell apart. His whole trip . . . is bullshit. He's a liar and a con man just like the rest of us. Just like you."

"Thanks for the tip," Stone said as he handed the controls over to the Mafia lord. "It makes everything . . . a little easier." Stone climbed up to the hatch and exited. He jumped down from the edge of the tank and headed up a small hill about a half mile from the fort. He stared through his binocs, lying flat on his stomach, and watched for about five minutes—setting in his mind just where the guards were moving, and the speed of the searchlights that slowly swept back and forth across the wide fields that surrounded Fort Bradley. He would go in from the back, where he knew it was slightly less guarded. When one of the floods had just made its back-and-forth route past his hiding place Stone leapt out and ran straight for the wall as fast as his feet could carry him. It was four in the morning. Stone knew how it worked in Fort Bradley—those men in the observation towers would have been on sixteen-hour, perhaps twenty-four-hour shifts. There was a tremendous shortage of manpower lately as Patton had had the men working eighteen-hour days preparing an invasion force to sweep over the countryside. They'd exhausted. If Stone could just move fast. Real fast.

He rushed through the dark funnel of shadows created by the lights reaching the ends of their sweeps a hundred yards apart on each side of him. Just ran as if he were sprinting the last hundred yards in the Olympics. Suddenly one of the beams was heading back toward him and he dove flat onto the ground, turning his head away so nothing would reflect off his dark camouflage flak jacket and pants. The search played over him for about ten seconds and then moved on. Hearing no gunfire or yells of intruder, Stone jumped up and was on full blast in just steps. He made it to the base of the fence and again flung himself flat on the ground as the lights turtled past. Stone knew from something the general had let slip when he had been drunk the other night that there was a section of fence ten feet long that was not electrified and that could be opened by merely releasing a catch. It was a quick-escape option for the general, should things explode. Only Stone was going to use it to break in.

He moved carefully along the bottom of the fence and found what he thought was the right section, without the little ceramic-coned electrical transformer on the other side and reached out a tentative hand. He touched the metal . . . and nothing happened. Stone rose carefully, searching for the release latch. He was directly below one of the guard towers now and suddenly heard pacing on the wooden platform fifty feet above him. Someone snorted in hard, far above, and then spat out a gob that landed on Stone's boot. He didn't move an inch. The spitter let out a contented snort and walked back to his chair, where he fell almost instantly into a doze.

Stone found the gate release and lifted it slowly. It made the slightest click and then the fence moved and Stone slipped through, closing it quickly behind him. He ran into the shadows created by the nearest warehouse and then started down one of the side streets of the fort. He knew his Harley was being stored in the main repair garage in the eastern part of Bradley and moved through the center of the fort, clinging to walls, edging around corners. There were always patrols, and who knew what other traps Patton might have set. But he made it to the garage without being spotted, a two-story building with the middle floor ripped out to create a thirty-foot-high space for the lifts to operate.

He entered through one of the back doors—it wasn't locked—and let his eyes adjust to the dim light of the few orange bulbs that were on here and there. There were tires, and frames, bumpers and engines everywhere, in various states of disassembly. Stone prayed that they hadn't done anything drastic to the Electraglide. It had kind of become his security blanket. But he was only about halfway through the place, walking on tiptoes as he though he heard strange clicking sounds everywhere, when Stone saw a row of ten motorcycles along one wall. His eyes lit on the Harley instantly and he rushed toward it, trying to see what shape it was in. And as he reached it and stopped just in front of it Stone was slightly amazed to see that it was in perfect shape. Even the machine gun and Luchaire mini-missile system built into the bike had been left untouched. They had probably just wheeled it in the day they brought him into camp with the intention of studying it further, and then had just forgotten about it. He looked close; there was still surface scum from the flood dried onto the seat and body. Not a hand had been laid on it.

. Stone sat down on the seat and pushed the instant start. The Harley came to life with a dull roar and he let it settle down before clicking it into gear. He moved slowly out of the garage and back around the corner into one of the darker streets, driving with the lights off. There was just one thing left to do. He headed toward the pound.

Stone could smell the animals blocks before he actually reached the place. He was downwind and the thick animal scents mixed pungently into the moist air. He turned the engine to neutral, letting himself glide the last few hundred feet, which angled slightly downward. Stone came to a stop just feet from the building and jumped off the bike in a flash, letting the autostand snap out and hold the Harley up. He was running out of time. He opened the side door and slipped inside to the huge animal pound and the rows of pens and cages spreading off as far as the eye could see. Blue light bulbs lit the scene with a dull light as Stone made his way carefully inside. He could hear the snores and slobbering, the sudden growls in sleep, the scratching and farting of over a thousand animals. He headed toward where he remembered the dogs were penned at the far end of the place, praying that he wouldn't set the place to barking when one little turd of a poodle woke up and started squealing shrill poodle barks. But they only lasted a few seconds, until Stone was out of range, and the thing settled back down into sleep.

Then he saw Excaliber, lying with his face pressed tightly between the bars of his holding pen. If he had once seemed content in his little prison—the last time Stone had seen him—he sure as hell had had a change of mind. The animal looked positively forlorn, its ears down at their sides, its eyes drooping down at both ends with a most depressed expression. Even the dog, given all the food it could eat, wanted its freedom more. Stone suddenly emerged from the shadows and the pitbull's eyes lit up as if they'd hit paydirt on a slot machine. The demonic white face pressed harder against the bars as if it had forgotten it couldn't go through them and it let out a whine that quickly grew in intensity until it threatened to turn into a siren.

"Shh, shh, dog, quiet," Stone whispered harshly through the blue half-darkness. "I've come to rescue your goddamned ass; don't get me killed." The pitbull clawed wildly at the bottom of the metal bars but kept its mouth shut, getting at least part of the message. Stone kneeled down beside the pen. "Little bastard. I shouldn't even rescue you. Thought you liked army life. Don't mind living in a cage the rest of your life." The canine gave him a hard squinting look that said cut the bullshit or I start barking and Stone searched for the catch on the cage. Only there wasn't any.

"You won't find it down there, Colonel Stone," a voice said suddenly from behind him. Stone rose with a sinking feeling in his gut. He turned slowly, wondering how long it would take him to reach the Uzi autopistol hanging around his shoulder or the Ruger .44 strapped inside his jacket, which he'd taken from the Harley. Too long, he could see as he came face to face with a chrome-plated .45. And Sergeant Zynishinksi who held it.

The sergeant looked at Stone through the blue luminosity of the gray air. "All the pens are controlled electrically from this panel here." The sergeant's other hand rested just above a long row of buttons set on a wide control panel built into the wall.

"Well, why don't you just press the button for number 257," Stone said as he read the number off the front of Excaliber's cage. "And I'll just get my dog out as General Patton promised I could after the last mission. Didn't he tell you?" Stone asked, dripping sincerity.

"It's all over, Stone. I know what's happening. You're setting us all up. I had my own man in on your operation, Sergeant Ferris. He was supposed to contact me every six hours and the messages stopped half a day ago. Stopped *after* you had signalled the general that the bosses had agreed to surrender. You shouldn't even be here. According to your message you were working out surrender technicalities down there and needed more troops. And yet here you are, sneaking into camp."

"I can explain," Stone said, slowly moving his foot to the right as he set himself to dive into the shadows created by a large water trough set in the center of the room several yards away.

"Explain, shit," Sergeant Zynishinksi spat in disgust. "A traitor to your own people. After the general promoted you above all his others, after I trained you." A look of real pain came over his granite face for a second. "I should have known from the skills you showed that you weren't the regular asshole. You knew too much. Way too much."

"Look, Sergeant," Stone said, moving fractions of an inch at a time, keeping one eye peeled on the pistol to see if it wavered even a millimeter. "I like you. Believe it or not. The training was . . . interesting, and I learned a lot of things from you. But I tell you, General Patton, although he is a brilliant general and a good soldier, is wrong. The world he would create is a nightmare, more like Hitler's dreams than Washington's, more like Stalin's slave camps than Lincoln's free society."

"And your own father was a military man of such great honor," the sergeant said with a sad shake of his head. "To have a son who would betray his country to a bunch of scum-sucking pigs."

"My father only said one thing to me about choosing sides," Stone said, his voice like ice, his face flushed, a little angry at the insults. "And that was to fight only for that which made men more free, not that which enslaved them more. I've made my choice."

"And chose to die," Sergeant Zynishinksi yelled, his whole face suddenly contorting in rage at the betrayal he felt by Martin Stone. He pulled the trigger hard but Stone was already in motion. He sprang off his coiled legs right through the air the moment the D.I. pulled the trigger. By the time the first .45 slug reached him it found only air. Stone hit the ground hard and rolled behind the water trough without stopping. The second he came to a rest, he ripped out the .44 Ruger and hefted it in his hand. It felt good to have his own firepower back in his hands after all the standard and substandard weaponry of the NAA. The .45 barked twice more, little puffs of dirt puffing up just a few feet away. The dogs were already starting to bark. Stone ran in a half crouch behind the trough as Sergeant Zynishinksi came in low on the other side and hit his last shot on the pistol. Stone stood up in a flash, leveling the thirteen-inch Redhawk at the sergeant, right between his eyes from about a foot away. The big man's own freshly loaded pistol still hung at his side.

"Don't make me do it," Stone said softly. "Don't make me kill you. You're basically a good man. Leave now, and raise a family, live somewhere out in the forests away from the rot and decay of humanity."

"You dare ask me to betray my men, the Third Army. You're an insult to the very uniform you wear, Stone. I'd rather die in my boots than sully the honor of Patton's Fighting Third." Stone saw his eyes tense up and he pulled the trigger as he closed hisown eyes. When he opened them, the sergeant didn't have a face anymore. Only he was still standing. The bloody, gouged-out hole that had once been where his nose stood was now just a pit of dripping gray brain matter oozing down over his lips, his chest, like the thick frothy water that boils off rice. Then the sergeant's dead knees collapsed together and the corpse fell to the ground like a straw scarecrow suddenly losing its nail on the pole. "Son-of-a-bitch," Stone whispered down at the spasming body. Not that he or anyone could hear the words. For the whole place had awakened from the gun battle and every dog, cat, laboratory rat and other non-human guest was letting loose with its own ear-splitting and repetitive squeals of fear and anger. The result was quite loud.

CHAPTER
Twenty-One

BUT IT got even louder as Stone heard the first whistling cannon shell fly overhead and erupt in a thunderous roar several blocks away. He looked at his watch. They were a half hour ahead of schedule. Either they had double-crossed him, or they'd heard the shooting and decided to go for it. Stone ran over Sergeant Zynishinksi's body and frantically scanned the release panel on the wall. At last he found the number and pulled it and Excaliber's cage snapped open with a ping. This time the dog flew out and ran to Stone, where it rubbed its head against his leg by way of thanks. Stone looked around at the other barking and squealing animals. They'd all be consumed in the firestorm that was about to descend. They hadn't done shit. He searched for the master release switch and found it.

"Get ready to move, dog," Stone said, pointing toward the front of the place, "'cause the fur is about to fly." He pressed the button hard and there was a loud whirring sound.

Suddenly every gate in the animal holding center opened and a flood of fur, fangs, claws and stiff tails such as the world has never seen erupted onto the floor. Stone and the pitbull made their way at full speed back through the warehouse, just linebacking their way through whatever got in the way. By the time they reached the back door the tank attack had begun in earnest and jeeps were already roaring around the base, men running around tucking in their shirts as they slammed magazines into their rifles. Stone leaped atop the Harley, turned it on, kicked into gear, all in one motion. He felt the weight of the pitbull land on the back of the bike and started forward at full throttle, doing a half wheelie before the front end slammed down and shot ahead.

Stone glanced around for a split second as they started down one of the streets and a smile streaked across his mouth as he saw the tidal wave of animal life pouring from every opening of the warehouse. The terrified creatures quickly spread out through the city on a mad dash for freedom, running through the legs of the rushing men, beneath the wheels of the streaming vehicles. The rats were deserting the ship and nothing better get in their way.

Stone headed toward the general's quarters as shells began going off everywhere. The crime bosses *had* been able to fire the damned things after all. From what he could see, the barrage was coming from all three sides of the fort, unrelenting, shell after shell, sending up whole buildings at a time. A blast went off just ten yards to the right of Stone and he nearly went over but caught the bike with the weight of his leg, pushed with everything he had on his boot, skidding along the asphalt, and righted the Harley without falling. The artillery units of the fort located at numerous sites around the encampment began opening up and soon shells traveling in both directions virtually filled the air overhead as if it were D-Day, or something pretty damned close to it.

Suddenly there was a terrific explosion at the north end of the camp, in one of the munitions buildings, that shook the road beneath the Harley. A ball of flame shot out hundreds of feet in every direction as a tower of burning debris flew straight into the sky as if Vesuvius were once again erupting. Vehicles careened by wildly all around him, but no one paid Stone any attention. In the smoke and flames already rising everywhere, it was hard to tell who anyone was.

He reached the corner that turned toward the general's headquarters and slowed down to a halt. Moving the bike an inch at a time he peered down the street toward where he knew there were machine-gun emplacements. But now, there was just smoking ruins. The entire building had taken not one but two hits at each end. Burning timbers, flaming masterpieces, melting sculpture lay in smoking fragments everywhere. Stone edged the bike slowly down the street, his hand on the trigger of the .50 caliber machine gun built in above the front fender. Not that it looked like much of anything could have survived the blasts. But as if to prove him wrong once again, a figure coated in black ash rose from the ruins, and whipped up a rifle, taking a bead on Stone. He slammed his finger down on the bike's handlebar trigger and the bike shook slightly back on its shocks as ten slugs big enough to take out an elephant slammed into the man, sending him spinning backwards like a top. Stone got off the bike and walked forward, searching for the body.

He saw it lying between two burning beams, the flames just starting to lap at its arms and legs. Stone stared down, and felt his stomach turn as the ripped apart, bloody thing on the ground moved its lips, tried to speak.

"He's not dead, Stone. The general escaped. And all your

traitorous plans will fail. Patton is at the missile silo now, and he's going to punch in the coordinates of Fort Bradley. We'll all die. All die together." The blood-coated face coughed and a gush of red liquid came rushing out. Then it sank down like the good dead thing that it was into the ground, into the dark soil that would be its home for the next billion years.

CHAPTER
Twenty-Two

S TONE PUSHED the Harley to the max as he shot
down the street that led out of the fort. All around him
Fort Bradley was covered with dancing sheets of yellow and red flame and secondary explosions every few seconds as a shell or pile of them went up. The tanks in the
attack force were still sending down a cyclone of shells
without letup, just sweeping their huge cannons back and
forth over every square inch of the place. The NAA troops
for their part sent back volleys of artillery and even missiles
from a multiple launch rocket system. But they had no targets to sight up and their shells exploded in the woods all
around the attack force, blowing up trees into flaming tooth-
picks, but not striking one of the tanks.

Suddenly he saw her coming through the smoke just off
the side of the street like a ghostly apparition. Stone pulled
both brakes hard and the Harley came to a skidding stop,
doing a one-eighty just feet from Elizabeth.

"Martin . . . what's happening . . . they said you were a traitor. They said—"

"Get on!" Stone barked. He couldn't go through his philosophical arguments again with tank shells landing just yards away.

"I—I can't," she said, sobbing, putting her hands to her face. "They said you—"

"Oh for Christ's sake," Stone screamed in exasperation. "If you want to hate me, fine, but stay alive to do it, okay? You'll be dead in another minute if you keep standing there." A 120mm came whistling down into the rooftop of a warehouse just across the street from them and they were almost knocked down by the force of the blast. But it seemed to make up her mind and she ran to the bike.

"Get on right behind me," he yelled over the roar of the firefight. "The dog can fit behind you." She pulled her leg over the leather seat in back of Stone, as Excaliber, looking a little chagrined by the musical seats, squeezed back as far as he could until his furry back was up against Stone's rack section on the rear of the Harley. Stone checked to make sure that everyone was basically on, and shot down the street as another shell sent the asphalt they had just been standing on up into a ball of superheated tar. He pushed the bike hard and it flew over bodies, past flaming tanks. A few NAA soldiers recognized him and let fly with a volley of rifle shots, but the Harley was already gone into the swirling mists of oily black smoke.

At last he saw the main gate ahead and the two machine guns set up, ready for an infantry assault. But they were aimed forward, and Stone was coming from behind. Without even stopping to really think about it—or he might not have —Stone accelerated and as Elizabeth buried her head in the back of his leather jacket, the Harley shot into the emplace-

ments. The bike slammed into two troops, sending them flying, and then the front wheel hit some sandbags. The Harley
seemed to almost take off, as if it had gone off a ski jump
ramp, and came down with a wicked slam about thirty feet
outside the fort. Stone ripped the wheel to the right and the
whole bike tilted over at a forty-five degree angle as they
veered off. The 9mm slugs of the machine guns burped out
death but the slugs raced into the air just behind the Harley.
And within seconds he was out of the line of fire.

Stone waited until he was about a quarter mile from the
fort and then stopped the bike.

"Last stop, baby," he said, turning around to her.

"You've taken me from there," she said, looking back at
the flaming maelstrom that had been the place she lived for
two years. "I have nowhere else to go. Take—take me with
you."

"I can't," Stone said softly. "I have to do something—
right now. And the chances are I won't be coming back. I've
got to go . . . now . . . I'm sorry." She dismounted and stood
by the bike, looking into his eyes with tears filling her own.

"Come back for me, Martin Stone. Please come back."
Stone managed a narrow smile, and then without a word was
gone.

He tore down the road that led to the silo, hunched far
over onto the bike as the dog hung on for dear life behind.
He prayed he would be in time. The results were too horrible
to contemplate. Somehow Stone didn't want to die in a burst
of atomic fire. He didn't like the idea. A knife, a gun: he
could deal with that, though he in no way sought it, but to
have your atoms themselves burnt down into . . . nothing—
just super-heated neutrons or something spinning through
space. The thought gave him shivers in the very depth of his
bowels.

He hit eighty, even ninety on the straightaway and was about halfway there when it began to snow. Oh Christ, was it going to be one of those nights, Stone thought with apprehension, starting to tighten up inside in knots of growing fear. The snow, although not dense, was cold and thick, wide crystalline flakes that were big enough to make a small meal when they landed on the lips or tongue. They quickly coated the road and the land around him, dusting it all with a shimmering blanket of white, pure, innocent, unstained white. It was beautiful, in a way, Stone thought coolly as he had to slow the bike to fifty to avoid skidding. It reminded him of when he had been a child and had had one of those bottles with Santa and all eight reindeer inside it and when you shook it the sky filled with the white snow, obscuring everything. Stone had always wondered if that's what it would look like after an atomic blast; if the fallout would drop down in thick sticking flakes like that, like tonight. Maybe it was the night to die after all. It sure as hell had the table settings for it.

He reached a fork in the road. Shit, he hadn't remembered a fork at all. He stopped the bike, looked back and forth for almost a minute, prayed and went to the right. Everything headed to the right. Everyone knew that. He had gone about ten miles and was just starting to be sure that he had the wrong direction when he saw the fenced-in silo ahead in the pale morning light that was just starting to trickle down through the sea of flakes that now filled the slate-gray sky. He had scarcely pulled within thirty yards of the front gate when a voice boomed over a loudspeaker.

"Hold where you were, unless you want to die!" a voice yelled out over a P.A. system. "What business do you have here?"

"I've got no time to explain," Stone said, knowing these

fellows were not about to let him in no matter what he had to
say. He jumped from the Harley and before they quite realized what he was doing Stone already had the Luchaire
89mm missile tube unlocked and pulled free from the side of
the bike. He aimed dead center between the two sandbagged
machine-gun nests, forward right through the wire-mesh
fence.

"Jesus, he's got—" the voice screamed over the micro-
phone and one of the big tripod-mounted 9mm's started to
fire, a row of slugs scissoring across the hard-packed dirt
toward the Harley. Stone pulled the trigger of the missile
launcher and the rocket screamed out of the front like something searching for blood. A tail of flame shot out the back
of the hollow firing tube. The Luchaire 89mm found what it
was looking for. The missile, designed to blow out the sides
of even the biggest tank, landed right between the two gun
posts and the whole world went up in a hailstorm of red and
yellow, sending all ten men flying up into the air like bowling pins hit by a sledgehammer. The blood of the blasted
dead splattered out onto the snowy ground, creating a wild
pattern of bright red drips and splatters in the sheer white
surface.

Stone ran toward where he remembered the steel door in
the ground to be and searched frantically around for the handle. Deep in the soil beneath him he swore he felt subsonic
rumblings as if the earth itself were about to vomit. Suddenly he found something and pulled hard and the steel door
swung up. At that very instant the ten-foot-wide alloy-steel
dome that covered the top of the silo began whirring and
opening down the middle. The two sides of the nearly im-
pervious steel slid smoothly and slowly apart, disappearing
down into wide slots in the concrete circle around them.

Stone lowered himself into the entrance and shot down the

rung ladder hand over foot as he heard the missile stirring, things clicking everywhere below him. Suddenly he heard another sound above, barking. Excaliber had followed him to the edge and right on in after him, not quite realizing the distance to be covered inside. As Stone looked up the yelping dog came flying down toward him like a meteor of fur. He caught the animal on his chest and they both went careening down the shaftway, bouncing back and forth between the ladder and the curved solid wall of the missile shaft behind them like ping pong balls. Stone felt himself hitting the bottom hard and then blacking out for a flash. He came to in what couldn't have been more than a second to find himself entangled in the squealing pitbull's legs. It pulled itself free almost immediately, stood upright and looked at him with a hangdog expression. It knew it had fucked up.

Stone didn't have time for reprimands. At least his arms and legs still worked. He walked around the base of the towering missile as the covering far overhead completely opened and locked. If the fucking thing fired now, Stone thought, standing only yards from the base of the rocket, he'd be BBQ before he had time to scream. He walked around the circular walkway as far from the towering atomic missile as he could—as if it mattered. Stone reached the shielded door to the control room and carefully lifted his head to the Plexiglas window. They were in there, Patton and the two technicians. The general was screaming at them and they were pushing dials and buttons and shit all over the place. Firing time had definitely arrived. Stone took two grenades he had grabbed from the dead suckers upstairs and looped them together with his belt. He hung it over the handle of the door and pulled both pins, rushing back around the base of the missile as the spear of high tech steel started shaking violently.

"Come on, dog, come on," Stone screamed as the animal trotted along slowly behind. But it got the message at the last second as it saw that Stone kept running, and it picked up a little speed, just enough to avoid the deafening blast that went off right around the bend. A shock wave flew past them on all sides and Stone felt some sharp stings in his legs and back as a few pieces of mini shrapnel dug like whirling saw blades into his flesh. He rose and ran back through the swirling dust of the silo and saw that the grenades had popped the lock. The door was ajar. Pulling the Ruger, Stone crossed himself with the pistol, kicked the door open and rushed into the control room.

"So, it is you," General Patton glared at him with utmost contempt as he stood toward the far end of the blinking and beeping missile control center. "I thought just perhaps they'd broken you, but I see now your greed extended far beyond what I had to offer. I misjudged your ability to even sell out your fellow countryman."

"I don't have time to explain, General," Stone said wearily. "I do what I do. Stop the missile and I won't pull the trigger of this .44 mag, which will take your head off if I do." He raised the Redhawk in a slow arc toward the general's face.

"Sorry, Stone, but I don't think so," the general sneered and snapped his fingers. In the excitement and the smoke Stone hadn't even noticed the white shape sitting at the general's feet. But he did now as Hannibal, Patton's eighty-five-pound pitbull, almost identical in appearance to Excaliber, raced down the long tiled floor toward Stone with a look of total annihilation on his snarling wild face. Before Stone could even move his arm to get the canine in his sights—he knew as he tried that he could never do it in time—another shape launched itself into the air from behind him. Excaliber, his own jaws opened to full like a shark, ready to take on the whole fucking world, flew past Stone. The two fighting dogs met in midair and crashed together to the floor. Excaliber was the first one up, spinning around on his side and he clamped down instantly on his adversary's leg, pulling it hard toward him so the dog couldn't gain its balance or rise. Hannibal snapped at the air with loud vicious chomps but couldn't find anything as Excaliber just kept pulling it around in a circle. Suddenly the pitbull chomped extra hard and the leg cracked in two. As Hannibal let out a howl of pain, Excaliber lifted his head and came down on the exposed neck. Again he clamped with all his might, his second eyelids closing protectively over his eyes as they always did on a full attack. He bit down hard, the jaws locking in place and then spun the dog back and forth in the air like a rag doll. The incisors tore through the thick muscle sheath around the neck of Patton's pitbull and into the pumping artery just inside. Hannibal howled like a siren as his neck opened up and a geyser of blood exploded out into Excaliber's face. Both their white coats were coated with red in just seconds.

Then, just as quickly, it was over. Excaliber shifted the neck in his jaws slightly, getting a deeper grip, crunched hard again and that was that. The spinal cord of the animal had been snapped in two. It fell to the floor of the control room, good for a bathroom rug and not much else.

Stone ripped up the Ruger, searching for Patton, but he had disappeared. A door at the far end where the general had been standing stood open. The technicians were still playing with buttons and Stone screamed at the top of his lungs, firing toward the closest one.

"Stop, stop, you fucking fools!" He hit the near man in the shoulder and he slumped over hard in his seat, held in place by the chains that locked him there for his shift. Then Stone turned toward the other. But the man had already risen. He was pointing toward the silo on the other side of the thick control room wall and laughing.

"It's too late, Colonel Stone, it's already launched." At the word "launch," Stone heard a roar like the world was going through the second coming, and the bulletproof Plexiglas window of the door, which had been closed, turned bright orange and filled with a sheer sheet of fire. The temperature of the control room shot up instantly and Stone felt himself covered with sweat. The whole place vibrated as if they were in an earthquake and Stone ran wobbly-legged toward the exit door through which the general had vanished.

The technician tried to grapple with him as he flew past but Stone thrust his pistol hand out and knocked the man back into his chair. He reached the door and saw that there was a back exit—this one steel-gridded circular stairs—that led right to the surface. Stone glanced around and saw the pitbull coming right after him. The thing looked a mess, covered in blood from nose to tip of tail, but it was something else's blood. The pitbull gave him a look of I-know-I-fucked-up-before-but-that-was-pretty-good-huh? and then bolted up the stairs behind him. As they reached the halfway mark Stone heard a deafening roar, then saw a sheet of flame pulsing through the exit door below. So much for technician number two.

But it was all too late. Stone knew that as he tore up the stairs, his boots almost skidding off the gridded steps as he flew along so furiously he could hardly keep his balance. It was too fucking late. The damage was done. He could feel the walls just the other side of him that encased the silo, shuddering like they were giving birth. The missile was rising, coming out of its hole in the ground, right alongside of him, rising like a tree on fire from the dirt. Still he ran, not wanting to die down here in a dark pit, even if he would soon enough be ashes.

He reached the cover at the top and pushed something titled EMERGENCY ESCAPE RELEASE. There was a loud burst of air and the round hatchway just above his head flew to the side, letting in the snow and the gray morning air. Stone flew from the exit and saw that he was about twenty yards behind the silo. The missile was rising out of the top of it, its flaming rockets just clearing ground level. It moved along achingly, grudgingly, as if it couldn't quite get up the energy to make it. But Stone knew these big ones took a few seconds to really pour it on. They had the ponderous strength of moon rockets, and rose almost lazily at first.

But even as Stone stood back, shielding his eyes from the burning cloud of smoke that spat out the bottom, the missile began gaining speed up into the purple-splattered dawn. God, God, he couldn't let it take off . . . though it was impossible to stop it. He scanned the back of the shielded enclosure around the silo and saw something—an antiaircraft gun. Stone tore over to it and grabbed the controls. It was an undamaged twin 35mm aircraft cannon. The thing looked like it would work. It was manually controlled—with an antique-type operation at that—with two small wheels for turning horizontally and vertically. Stone jumped into the metal bucket seat built behind the weapon and spun the wheels for all he was worth. The entire gun system spun around smoothly on a complex gear system beneath the frame and within seconds Stone had the missile in his dish-sized sights.

The M-7 was about two hundred feet up now and accelerating by the second. It filled the air around him with a thundering roar as if the very gods were screaming out encouragement. For him or it, he didn't know. Stone pulled the trigger of the antiaircraft guns and held it down. It was as if he was on a brahma bull at the rodeo, only this was a rodeo of megadeath. The gun jerked and shimmied and did all kinds of strange little dances, as if it were trying to send Stone flying. But it also shot a weaving trail of screaming slugs up into the curtain of snow falling everywhere in the sky except just beneath the rocket, whose flaming thrust burnt a hole right through the snowflakes as it rose.

Stone couldn't see shit with all the smoke and thick flakes falling in his face. But he leaned back, following the tail of the thing, trying to send a stream right into the fiery tail. And suddenly he hit something. He knew the thing was hurt as it suddenly wobbled violently to the side, the whole rocket section vibrating back and forth wildly like a washing machine with too many clothes in it. Then the M-7 began spinning around like a top as pieces of metal and wire from its guidance system fell from the sky. The long tail of white flame sputtered and then went completely out. And as Martin Stone watched in happiness—and horror—the ten megaton missile began dropping right back down toward him.

"Jesus Christ," he whistled through his teeth. He hadn't thought about that one. He heard a barking sound and flashed a glance down at Excaliber, who was staring up at the smoking missile headed right toward them as if to say you-do-know-how-to-deal-with-that-right? kind of look that Stone found most unsettling. He stared back up again and saw that the thing was directly overhead, the tail section growing as large as the side of a house, coming down right on top of him. He threw his hands over his head, which he knew even as he did it was about the most absurd motion imaginable. As if his arms would protect him from the blast of a ten megaton hydrogen bomb going off at his hairline.

There was a tremendous ripping and crashing sound that seemed to occur what felt like an inch from Stone's nose, though he wasn't watching, since his eyes were shut tight as sealed crypts. The ground quaked violently, shaking the antiaircraft gun and the seat he was in all over the place like one of those crazy rides at an amusement park. Then it all seemed to settle down, with just the whooshing sound of the fire from the silo filling the air with an almost soothing hiss.

Stone opened his eyes. And couldn't believe them. The missile had crashed to earth not more than thirty feet away. It had come down almost as straight as an arrow, backwards, and the tail section of the M-7 was buried in the earth a good six feet deep. The dirt had extinguished what fire was burning so it just sat there smoking like a skyscraper of steel death as far from Stone as he could spit. He stared at the thing for long seconds and then got out of the antiaircraft chair and walked slowly over to it, the pitbull following cautiously behind. It didn't like the immense missile and snarled at it from between partially opened jaws.

The atomic weapon lay there dead, little streams of smoke drifting up all around it. It hadn't gone off. Stone could only think that the warhead was armed to detonate at a certain altitude. But it had never reached that altitude—and never would—lying here broken, useless. He looked suddenly around for General Patton. But the madman was already gone, his half-track tires disappearing in the snow through a back exit. And now Stone knew the son-of-a-bitch had two more of the H-missiles. And he'd use them. God, would he use them. Stone was going to have fucking A-bombs trying to find him all over Colorado. No matter what he did, things seemed to get worse. It couldn't get much worse than this. Could it?

Stone heard a sudden hissing sound and looked around. His face instantly lit up like a Christmas tree and he felt a surge of love for the dog that almost made it all worthwhile. For the animal had walked to the very base of the hundred-foot ICBM, lifted its back right leg and proceeded to send out a pungent stream of piss onto it. A little cloud of steam rose above the pitbull as the liquid hit the still sizzling hot metal of the steel tail. Stone laughed out loud into the snowy air. And then laughed again. Never had a dog had such a fire hydrant to raise its leg to. And Stone knew that for the pitbull, there could be no greater reward than that.

CHAPTER
Twenty-Three

"COME ON, dog," Stone said wearily, turning and walking away from the immense steel spear of megadeath immovably imbedded in the ground like King Arthur's sword as swirls of cottony snow fell from the sky. "Let's get the hell out of here before we start glowing or get our fucking chromosomes all twisted and rearranged." There was something about standing right next to so much potential destruction that gave Stone the shivers. And he wasn't quite convinced that the thing wouldn't go off at any moment. Excaliber let loose a final stream of steaming liquid and then put his leg back down. He sniffed at the ICBM for a few seconds, his moist black nose opening and closing as he tested the air for his own territorial marking scent. Then the pitbull turned, snapping his head up and away with a motion of contempt, as if it was he who had emasculated the missile, and ran over to the

Harley and up onto the back seat, where he wrapped his muscular legs around the snow-dusted leather.

Stone started the bike up and headed out through the silo perimeter fence, a large section of which had been blasted apart by the Luchaire 89mm and hung in twisted steel tatters on its side like the jaggedly opened top of a sardine can. He drove into the white mists without a look back. It took hours to reach the outskirts of Fort Bradley, although even through the curtains of snow he could see the rising funnels of black smoke from miles away, hear the explosions still going off everywhere. The attack rages on, though it was now unclear just who was fighting who. The whole battle had seemed to have deteriorated into pure anarchy as bullets, artillery and tank shells streamed through the air like the fourth of July. The bastards were after the spoils now. The Mafia and the Guardians of Hell and the mountain bandits and the filth-coated slime who were beyond description were closing in on the fortress itself, wanting to grab up the booty of war, the heavy firepower that every man was doubtless thinking would make him king of the hill back in whatever shithole he called home.

"Good." Stone spat as he watched the conflagration, saw the sky painted orange and red for miles above the fort. "Let them wipe each other out." The less of the whole sick crew that was left, the better the rest of humanity would fare. Still, he had no illusions that they would complete the job. The toughest would survive. And they would take every bit of death-dealing firepower they could carry, to further their greedy little ambitions. Still, a lot of them were dead. And most important, Stone had destroyed Patton's Reich before it had a chance to take root. He had given mankind a little more breathing room before the thousand-year darkness closed in.

And somewhere inside him, inside the pain and the disgust at so much death, inside the deep depression that he could feel threatening to overwhelm him from inside, Stone felt a certain dark joy that he had stopped the madman from turning America into an endless concentration camp. As bad as things were, men were still free. Free to fight, free to forge their own slovenly existences in the midst of the wastelands and the human predators. Hardly a chance in hell perhaps, but nonetheless, in some indefinable but terribly important way, they were free.

Then he saw Elizabeth lying in the snow. And whatever slim slivers of hope had been coursing through his veins vanished like a gob of spit in the hard ice-coated ground. She was prone, face forward in the white snow, her blonde hair spread out around her head. She lay right where he had seen her last. Right where she had looked at him with those pitiful doe eyes and said, "Come back for me, Martin Stone. Come back." And even from several hundred yards off Stone knew she was dead. He could feel it in every cell in his body and he felt a wall of tears start to rise up inside him.

Suddenly his face twisted into a grimace of sheer hatred. For as he watched, two black-jacketed bikers came roaring out of the fortress gates and skidded to a stop just feet from her. He could see by the way they nearly fell from their bikes and staggered through the snow that the bastards were drunk as skunks. They bee-lined straight for her, bent on having their sick pleasure. Dead or alive, it didn't matter to them. Didn't matter if she was hot or cold, just fuck 'em all like they were human garbage.

Stone roared the Harley forward as he heard the bull terrier growling hard on the seat behind him. He shot down the icy road heedless of going over, his mind filled with a boil-

ing rage that felt like his skull would explode right into the
flake-filled air. He saw one of the bikers drop his pants and
start to lower himself down on her, but he never reached his
sick goal. Stone's fingers found the trigger of the .50 caliber
machine gun mounted on the front of the Harley and he held
it down hard. The hail of screaming slugs tore through the
air and struck paydirt, flinging the half crouched biker backward through the air like a rag doll, his bullet-riddled body
rolling over and over in the snow. And as his pal reached for
a nickel-plated .45, his eyes wide as saucers, Stone swiveled
the bike slightly and ripped the bastard in two, his guts
spewing out over the pristine white ground, soiling it with a
stench beyond death.

Stone skidded to a halt just yards from her and jumped off
before the Harley had completely stopped, its auto kickstand
snapping out as an internal mechanism sensed the lack of
weight on the seat. He rushed over to her and kneeled down
by her side. And slowly, almost unable to bear the feel of
her cold flesh, he turned her over. She hardly looked real.
More like a china doll, a princess from some child's story-
book. Her cheeks were so white, white as the snow that
surrounded her, her lips like fading rosebuds that had
dropped from the vine before they had ever reached their full
beauty. Then he saw the small circle of blood, starkly red
against her blonde hair. Just under the right ear, a hole
hardly wider than a pencil, the blood already frozen over the
wound so hardly any had poured out, just a few droplets on
the snow beneath her head. It hardly seemed possible that
such a small hole in her flesh could have such terrible results. But Stone had been around it enough now to know that
death could enter through the smallest of doors.

Then he saw the note, a small piece of lined paper, pro-
truding from her half unbuttoned jacket and his hand thrust

down, angrily ripping it from her body as if it were a foul
and alien presence near her snow white skin.

> Just a little thank-you note, Colonel Stone. You took
> what mattered most to me—so I take what is yours.
> But don't think that this evens us up. It doesn't. If it
> takes the rest of my life, I will destroy you. Will
> follow you, will find you wherever you flee. And I
> will kill you. Of that you can rest assured. And by
> the way, Stone, just so you fully comprehend the
> situation, there are more missiles. The countryside is
> filled with them. Silos with my men ready to fire
> whenever I give the word. So look over your
> shoulder, and look up at the sky, and look deep into
> every shadow. And never stop looking, because I'm
> hunting you, Martin Stone. Hunting you until I find
> you, and send you into hell in a blast of atomic fire
> that will leave not a trace of the greatest traitor that
> America has ever known.

> General Patton III

Stone crumpled the note with such fury that his nails dug
into his palm, leaving little tracks of red. Then he threw it
far into the frigid air so it landed near one of the still oozing
bikers. He leaned down over Elizabeth's motionless body
and mindlessly stroked her blonde hair over and over again.

"Oh baby, baby, I'm sorry, I'm sorry. You didn't deserve
this." He moaned the words in a voice so low that even he
could hardly hear them above the wind-driven snow and the
explosions that lit up the dark morning all around him. He
remembered how warm her body had been against his, how
sweet her whispers of passion in his ear. And now because

of him, she was nothing. He felt as if he were going mad, a wall of hate rising in one part of him and another equally powerful wall of infinite sadness welling up in another. And with tears dripping slowly from his eyes, falling down onto her pale cold face and running down her cheeks, as if it were she who were crying, Stone whispered to her.

"I'll find him, Elizabeth. If I die doing it, I will avenge you. I swear to whatever perverse god rules this sick world." But Stone knew the words were for himself and not her. For she could no longer hear a thing. And it took every bit of willpower in his tired and racked body not to lie down in the snow beside her and go to sleep, forever.

And More From
MAX BRAND

And More from
MAX BRAND